A Groom for Carrie

by

Marie Higgins

Copyright © 2020 Marie Higgins

All rights reserved.

ISBN- 9798569707027

THE BLIZZARD BRIDES

Welcome to Last Chance, Nebraska! When the freak blizzard of 1878 kills most of the men in a small Nebraska town, what does it mean for the surviving women and children? Realizing they need to find men of honor to help rebuild, the women place an advertisement in the Matrimonial Times. Choosing a husband is more difficult than they thought when there is an overwhelming response to the ad. Will these Blizzard Brides find the second chance at love in a town called Last Chance?

A GROOM FOR CARRIE

Carrie Porter doesn't know what she's lost until it's gone. With her husband dead, and a young child to feed, she must rely on herself to improve her situation… or find a wealthy husband to care for her desolate family. When she chooses a man looking for a mail-order bride, she prays he will be her salvation.

ONE

Nebraska 1878

What had once been Carrie Porter's salvation had now put her in the depths of hell.

Frowning, she glanced out the window of her home, not realizing until now how life had changed so drastically in a few months. It seemed impossible that only two and a half months ago, Last Chance, Nebraska, had received the worst blizzard in history. Four feet of snow had packed the land – twice – not only killing their crops and most of the animals, but the freezing temperatures had also taken the lives of some of the people in town. The greater number of those who'd died were men – husbands of the women in town. Carrie's own husband had perished, as well. She had relied heavily on him for support, and just like that, he was ripped right out of her life.

Five years ago, Michael Porter had taken her away from New York City and promised that they would live like kings. As newlyweds, they were in love and anxious to start a family, but they both decided that New York was not where they wanted to grow old together. When they found Last Chance, Nebraska, they felt this was their home.

Unfortunately, once Michael had opened up the town's first bank, he had spent so much time there that he ignored his wife, and when their first child came a few years later, he wasn't around to help her. Carrie knew he was trying to follow through with his promise of living like kings, which was why he was hardly ever home. However, it wasn't that terrible, considering Tilly, the maid she'd brought with her from New York, had been the one who showed Carrie how to be a mother. Tilly was also the one who kept food in their bellies and clean clothes on their backs. Since Carrie had come from a wealthy family, she'd had a maid growing up, and Tilly was a godsend.

Taking a deep breath, Carrie smoothed her palms down her blouse and further to the waist of her teal colored skirt. It wasn't until she had gotten word that Michael had been frozen during the blizzard when she realized how much she had relied on her maid. Tilly had helped Carrie mourn Michael's death, as well as assisted in caring for little Parker Joe.

Sadly, her son would never remember his father. But, if all went well this morning, she would have another man to marry who would take on husband and father titles and responsibilities.

Deep coughing from the other room brought Carrie out of her depressing thoughts. Poor Tilly had caught a chest cold over a month ago, and the middle-aged woman hadn't been able to shake it. Carrie moved away from the window and walked into the kitchen, where Tilly sat at the table, peeling potatoes. The woman's face was flushed, and moisture coated her forehead. Wisps of short, black hair along her temple stuck to her skin in certain areas.

"Tilly, you should really go lie down." Carrie moved to her maid and placed her hand on the woman's shoulder. "I will peel the potatoes."

Tilly arched a thick eyebrow as a grin touched her mouth. "The last time I gave you a knife, you nearly cut off your finger." She shook her head. "No, I'm going to make some soup, and you cannot stop me."

Irritation boiled inside Carrie. "If you don't take care of yourself, what good will you be? I need you well, Tilly. If you cannot think of my welfare, think of poor Parker Joe. He will starve if you're too sick to cook, and you don't want to be responsible for his starvation, do you?"

Tilly rolled her eyes. The older woman knew when Carrie was acting dramatic, and although she was this time, she was still trying to make her point on the subject.

"I'll go lie down, but only because Parker Joe is resting, too. Someone has got to watch him while you go collect yourself a new husband."

Carrie's chest tightened. It physically hurt to think of starting all over again with a new man in her life. But, it had to be done. Pastor Collins had told all of the mourning widows that they couldn't stay in Last Chance unless they all found new husbands. That was the very thing to push the women into action. They set up an ad in Grand Platte's newspaper, advertising for grooms.

It had surprised Carrie that so many men had responded, and she – along with the other widows – were able to choose their own man. Carrie picked Dr. L. C. Hamilton. She'd prayed the Lord would guide her toward the man who would not only rescue sick people in town but rescue her and Parker Joe, as well.

"Yes," Carrie said with a heavy sigh. "It's almost time to meet my future husband."

Tilly patted Carrie's arm. "Don't worry, child. He will get to know you and fall in love with you, just as Michael did."

Trying to smile through trembling lips, Carrie straightened her shoulders and nodded. "It would be wonderful to be in love again, but I fear it's too soon. I miss Michael so much." Her voice broke, and she quickly cleared her throat.

"As do I." Tilly nodded.

Carrie assisted her maid into the smaller bedroom to lie down. Tilly kissed Carrie's forehead and smiled weakly. "Don't worry about Parker Joe. He'll be just fine."

"I'm never worried about him when I know you're here."

Carrie walked out of the maid's room. Before leaving the house, she tiptoed to her son's room and peeked inside. He was still asleep in the crib. Thankfully, his room was still toasty warm.

Although the weather had warmed up considerably in three months after the freezing blizzard, there was still a nip in the air and snow on the ground since it was officially winter. She slipped into her black waist-coat and placed the matching hat with the single teal feather on her head. She always tried to look her best, even if she was considered still in mourning.

She left the house and briskly walked toward the church. The women in town had chosen the church to meet their prospective grooms. During the past two weeks, men had trickled in, and Pastor Collins had quickly officiated the marriage ceremonies. There were still many women waiting for their men, and although it had been grueling waiting for her special day, now that it was here, she was a nervous wreck.

Out of all the men who had responded to the newspaper ad, she had always liked the name Hamilton. When she was a young girl in pigtails and in school, there was a boy a year older who had teased her endlessly. He came from a prominent family, and their last name was Hamilton. Although the boy was a holy terror, she recalled having doe-eyes for his older brother. Of course, the silly crush didn't last long, but it was nice to dream. Thankfully, she'd forgotten about the mean brother, and she was relieved that his rotten attitude didn't sway her from liking his last name. She still felt it was a strong name, and soon… it would be hers.

Carrie Hamilton… Mrs. Doctor Hamilton.

She flexed her hands by her side and quickened her pace. It would be quite an adjustment not to introduce herself as Carrie Porter after today. And she prayed the good doctor would allow Parker Joe to take on that last name, as well.

As the church came into view, her heartbeat accelerated. She couldn't remember being so nervous before. Marrying Michael had been a dream-come-true. He'd courted her for three months, and they were in love. Entering marriage with him had been anticipated. But today… not so much. In fact, the wedding night scared her nearly to death.

When she reached the front door of the church, her body trembled so badly, she thought she might need someone to hold her up. She stopped before opening the door and inhaled deeply. Closing her eyes, she repeated in her mind, *you can do this, Carrie.* She wasn't the first woman in Last Chance to marry a stranger, and she wouldn't be the last. If those other women could do it, so could she.

Carrie just hoped that when the doctor discovered that she relied heavily on her maid to do everything around the house, he wouldn't regret his decision to marry her.

Straightening, she entered the church, holding her chin up. She couldn't appear frightened.

The pastor stood at the front of the chapel with another man, talking by the pulpit. The pews were empty, but the curtains were open wide, letting in the sunshine.

The small organ sat empty, and her fingers itched to play the instrument. It had been too long since she last played.

Holding her breath, she took slower steps as she studied the doctor's profile. From what she could see of him, he appeared to be around her age, maybe a little older. His sandy-brown hair fell down his neck, and he sported a trimmed mustache and beard that were the same color. He wore a nice long, black suit-coat, and on his slender legs were matching trousers.

The man chuckled at something Pastor Collins said, and the doctor's baritone voice sent her heartbeat skipping in rhythm. She'd always liked men with deep voices. Unfortunately, though, Michael's voice wasn't as deep.

Pastor Collins saw her first, and he smiled wide. "Mrs. Porter, please come closer and meet Mr. Hamilton."

Finally, her soon-to-be husband turned and looked at her. He was quite handsome, even with his facial hair, and as she neared him, she noticed his eyes were evergreen. She'd known a few people in her life with eyes that color.

She tried holding her smile steady as she looked at the doctor. "Good afternoon."

He took two steps closer as his gaze roamed over her, from the top of her head down to her black boots. When his gaze finally rested on her eyes, he nodded. "It's nice to finally meet you, Mrs. Porter."

Something tugged in the back of her memory. Had they met before? He looked somewhat familiar, but she couldn't figure out where they might have met. It must have been when she lived in New York before she was married. Yet, that seemed vague, too. It would drive her crazy until she remembered.

"You don't know how much I appreciate your willingness to help me out." She swallowed hard. "You are a godsend, Doctor Hamilton."

"When I read about what happened to this town, I felt this was where I needed to be."

"May I ask where you are from?"

"I went to college to study medicine in Peru, but I'm originally from New York."

Surprised, she gasped lightly. "Indeed? I'm from New York, as well."

His gaze narrowed on her, and it seemed he studied her closer this time. It didn't bother her, only because she was looking at him the same way. Yet, she still couldn't pinpoint where they would have met.

"What is your maiden name, Mrs. Porter?"

"Jones. My father was a lawyer."

His eyes widened, and his mouth hung open. This time when he looked her over, there was amazement in his expression. "Robert Jones is your father?"

At least she knew this man had been friends with her father. "Yes."

"You're Carrie Jones?" He shook his head. "The last time I saw you, you were climbing trees and playing in the mud."

She laughed lightly. "Well, I'm happy that you know me, but I'm still trying to place you. I've known a few Hamiltons when I was growing up, but I fear I cannot remember where we could have met."

His chest shook with silent laughter as he pushed his fingers through his hair. "I sat in back of you at school, and I pulled your pigtails. You knew me as Cade Hamilton."

Shock vibrated through her as memories from the past flooded her mind. Cade — the boy she'd hated because he teased her endlessly. The holy terror in school that was always standing with his nose in the corner of the room for misbehaving.

Inwardly, she groaned. And now he was going to be her husband?

Her heart raced in panic. Was it too late to withdraw the offer of marriage?

TWO

Cade Hamilton couldn't believe his rotten luck. Out of all the women he would end up with, why did it have to be that spoiled girl who irritated him when he was a boy? He couldn't put his finger on why he didn't like her unless it was because their teacher doted on Miss Carrie. He was certain it had something to do with her father being wealthy, while his father struggled to make a good living for his family.

However, it appeared that life's heartaches had changed her, too. She didn't look like the haughty little girl he remembered. Instead, she was a desperate woman who needed a husband.

He hesitated to continue with their plans, but this town had *called* to him. He'd been praying for the Lord to guide him in the direction he needed to take after deciding not to continue being a doctor. When he'd lost a patient due to his mistake, Cade realized that he'd chosen the wrong career. Now he wanted to be a farmer since that's what he'd been raised to do… and this poor town needed his help badly after suffering from the awful effects of the blizzard.

Apparently, the Lord had a sense of humor to want Cade to end up with the uppity girl from his past. Indeed, Cade would have to really curb his tongue while in her presence – at least until they became used to each other.

When she chuckled, he could tell it was forced. But from this point forward, they would be walking on eggshells around each other, so he should get used to it now.

"Yes, I do remember you, Cade Hamilton," she said.

He could tell from her tone of voice that she felt the same way about him as he felt about her.

"Splendid." Pastor Collins clapped his hands twice. "I'm happy to know that you two aren't total strangers."

Cade wanted to argue with the preacher because, really, they were still strangers.

"Then, without further ado," Pastor Collins continued, "let's start the ceremony." He withdrew a paper and ink pen. "Let's have you both sign the marriage certificate."

Carrie signed first. Her hand trembled when she handed the pen to Cade, and he wrote his signature. The preacher took the paper again and set it on the table. He then opened his Bible.

Holding his breath, Cade waited for Carrie to say something to stop the preacher from beginning. Her stiff body and pale face let him know that she wasn't very enthused about marrying him. Although he had doubt, he wouldn't let her ruin his chances of starting a new life here and helping out some of these poor women who needed help with their farms.

"Dearly beloved. We are gathered here today…"

Cade breathed slightly better the longer the preacher continued to recite the marriage ceremony. It didn't take long to get to the vows, and once again, Cade held his breath, waiting for her answer.

Carrie's throat jumped in what appeared to be a hard swallow. "I… will."

Inwardly, he sighed, trying not to make it apparent how on edge he was. Seconds later, it was his turn. "I will."

"By the powers invested in me by the state of Nebraska, I pronounce you husband and wife." The preacher paused, and his eyes widened. He quickly cleared his throat. "This is the moment when I usually say, *you may kiss the bride,*" he told Cade. "But due to the circumstances surrounding this event, I don't think—"

"Actually," Cade quickly said. "I don't think it'll hurt anything if I kiss the bride. After all, we know each other." He gave Carrie a wink and took her in his arms. She gasped and placed her hands on his chest as if she were going to stop him, so he hurried and pressed his mouth to hers.

She stiffened in his arms, but he wouldn't stop just yet. On the spur of the moment, he'd realized that having their first kiss would be the perfect time to break the ice between them. Their marriage would definitely be in name only, but he at least wanted to be friends with her.

It only took a few seconds, but soon Carrie's body relaxed. The hands resting on his chest didn't feel like claws any longer. In fact, her mouth softened, and her lips moved with his. Warmth filled him quickly, and a feeling he hadn't experienced for a while hit him full force. Why did he desire the woman he'd never liked as a child?

Warning bells rattled in his head as shock vibrated through him. This was not right, and it needed to be stopped now.

Cade knew that jerking back wouldn't be proper, so he gradually ended the kiss and pulled away. Her eyes were wide when their gazes met, and her cheeks bloomed with a bright color. He figured she was as shocked as he was at this moment.

"Well, um…" Pastor Collins cleared his throat. "I suppose congratulations are in order now."

Carrie blinked as if she were coming out of a daze. She looked at the preacher. "Thank you for performing the ceremony."

"Of course." He smiled. "I'm very happy you have decided to stay in Last Chance."

Cade wanted to ask Carrie why Pastor Collins had said that. Had Carrie thought of leaving after her husband died? But now was not the time. Cade would question her about it later.

"Well, Mr. Hamilton, if you would like to follow me, I'll show you to your new home."

Her voice cracked, and she blinked back tears, but her eyes continued to grow watery. Cade was sure she was thinking of her deceased husband. The transition to fill another man's shoes would be long and tedious, but if the Lord brought Cade here to help others, he would do all he could to get through this complicated process.

"Lead the way, Mrs. Hamilton."

He followed Carrie, and as they reached the door, he picked up one of his trunks and tossed it over his shoulder securely before lifting the second trunk. She gasped, her gaze jumping from one trunk to the other.

"Forgive me for not bringing a wagon," she said softly. "But I only have one horse, and he needs to be shoed."

"I can shoe the horse, so don't worry. But I don't need a wagon. I can walk." He glanced away from her, looking toward the town. "How far do you live?"

She pointed up the hill. "Not far, but it's an upward climb."

"I'm fine with that. I carried my trunks from the stagecoach to the church. I think I can handle walking to your house."

"If…" She cleared her throat again. "If you'd like, I could carry one."

"Sweetie, I don't think you are strong enough."

She squared her shoulders and lifted a chin. Now she reminded him of the little girl he had loved to tease

"Mr. Hamilton, I'm stronger than you think. And, although I might not be able to carry one by myself, I could at least help you carry that one." She pointed to the one in his left hand.

"Fine. Take the other end." He couldn't wait to see how long it would take before she lost her strength.

She bent and wrapped her fingers around the handle and lifted it up. They started walking up the hill in silence. He wondered if she would say anything about the kiss, but then, he wasn't sure if he had an excuse as to why the kiss had turned tender for that brief moment. Perhaps not talking about the kiss was the best action to take.

"Carrie, will you tell me why Pastor Collins thought you were going to leave town?"

She glanced at him before turning her attention back to the road. "After we all realized our husbands had died in the blizzard, Pastor Collins let us know that we shouldn't be living on the prairie unless we were married because we would be too much of a temptation to those few men who survived the blizzard. He suggested we travel east toward the big cities and look for new husbands there."

Cade scowled. "Well, I suppose he has a point, but it's none of his business to tell you and the other widows what you should or should not do."

She shrugged. "Pastor Collins does care about our welfare… in his own little way, I suppose."

"Did all the widows decide to stay and find husbands?"

"I'm not sure. I don't know of any that have left."

"Well, my heart goes out to all of you who suffered. Losing loved ones isn't an easy thing to overcome." His memory opened, and little Clarence's face popped into Cade's head. His heart wrenched. That little boy's family would forever be mourning because of Cade's mistake.

He shook off the memory and looked back at Carrie. Her eyes misted over again, but she kept her gaze on the road.

"I'm grateful that you didn't turn me down," he said meekly.

Her head snapped toward him. "What do you mean?"

"Well, considering how we felt about each other when we were young, I thought you would change your mind about the wedding."

"Yes, well... I realized that we have both grown up quite a bit. At least I know I have."

He chuckled lightly. "You have, and so have I."

"Good. I'm happy to know that."

They were nearly to the top of the small hill, and he was surprised that she hadn't complained yet. Perhaps she had grown up, after all.

"How long have you been a doctor, Mr. Hamilton?"

Inwardly, he cringed. Carrie didn't know about his career decision yet. He supposed now was a good time to inform her. "I think you should call me Cade since we're married."

She nodded.

"But to answer your question, I've been going to school for several years, and I've been working alongside a doctor. I've never had a practice of my own. However, a couple of weeks after I had decided to come here, something happened, which made me realize that I'm not cut out to be a doctor."

Her steps stopped suddenly. He had been expecting it, and so stopped with her. Carrie's eyes were wide, and her cheeks had grown red.

"You... didn't come to Last Chance to be a doctor?"

He shrugged. "Originally, I had. But as I'd mentioned a couple of weeks ago, something happened—"

"And you didn't feel the need to let me know sooner?"

He cocked his head, studying her face. She was upset, and he wasn't sure he liked it. "Carrie? Did you marry me because I was a doctor?"

"Well... of course." She huffed. "We need a doctor here in town. We have some midwives, but that's it." She shook her head. "Some people are sick, and they need medical help. We are in great need of your expertise." She sighed. "In fact, my maid, Tilly—"

"*Maid?*" Cade gasped, not believing what he just heard. "You have a... maid?"

Carrie glared at him. "Yes. I brought her with me from New York after Michael and I were married."

"You can actually afford to pay her salary?"

Carrie rolled her eyes. "It's not like that. She's more like family. She helps me. She always has, and I cannot live without her. Tilly is very sick, and I was hoping that you'd make her your first patient."

Cade bit his tongue, not wanting to get Carrie upset. He still couldn't comprehend that she'd bring her maid to the prairie. Then again, Carrie was raised far differently than he – or most children – were raised.

"I'll see what I can do for your maid, however," he took a deep breath, "I'm *not* going to be the town's doctor. You and the others had better pray they find another one."

Disappointment etched in her pretty face, and guilt snuck inside him. But he couldn't let her – or anyone else – make him do something he didn't want to do. Wasn't it enough that he was responsible for Clarence's death? He didn't want to be the reason someone else died.

THREE

Carrie struggled the last several steps toward the house. She didn't dare admit that Cade had been correct when he suggested his trunk might be too heavy for her to carry. She knew how he felt about her. He'd called her a spoiled brat enough times as a child, and it was obvious he still thought of her that way. Why else would he have sounded so surprised when she talked about her maid?

But that wasn't what had her upset. She couldn't believe Cade hadn't told her about his change in professions. If she had known he wasn't planning on being a doctor when he reached Last Chance, she would have picked another man to marry. She had told the other women in town that a doctor was finally coming to Last Chance. Now she had to eat her words.

Pain pounded in her head, and her limbs became weak, but she held strong. She didn't need him seeing her as being feeble, so she continued walking. They neared the front porch, and she couldn't hold up the trunk any longer. Her arm refused. Then again, her legs were refusing to move any further, as well.

As her fingers released the handle of the trunk, she took two more steps before she collapsed, falling on the snow-covered ground. A fog swam in her head, and sounds around her were muffled.

Cade's panicked voice called out her name. At least, that's what she thought he had said. As her head began to spin, she felt two strong arms around her, lifting her against his body. Her limbs were useless, but she fought for control. She wasn't certain what was happening to her, but it felt like a dream. Yet, this was like a nightmare.

The moment they were inside her house, the warmth circling around, and the familiar scents wafting through the air, calmed her slightly. Her head throbbed, and she moaned, wishing it would go away so that she could become fully alert.

Cade must have set her on the couch because a cushioned softness was against her back. As he continued to say her name, his cold hands moved over her face and into her hair. The pressure from her head lightened, and she guessed he had removed her bonnet.

Another voice was in the room. *Tilly*. Carrie's fears lightened considerably. Her maid would help.

Several moments later, a cold, wet rag was placed on Carrie's head. Seconds later, she smelled something rank that brought her alert. Her head pounded fiercely, but at least she felt that she had control over her body once again.

The first person Carrie noticed was Tilly standing at the end of the couch. The older woman's face was pale, and beads of moisture clung to the woman's forehead. The maid's eyes were tired, but relief was the expression on the woman's face.

"Welcome back," Cade said.

Carrie switched her focus to the man kneeling beside the couch. His gentle smile soothed her. "What... happened to me?"

"I think your body was trying to pass out, but your mind fought it. You were in and out." He motioned toward Tilly. "Thankfully, your maid had some smelling salts."

Carrie should bring up the fact that if *he* had come to town to be a doctor, as he led her to believe, then he would have smelling salts, too. But her pounding head stopped the words she wanted to say. "Yes, Tilly is a godsend."

"I think you need some food in your belly. That will help." Tilly turned and moved into the kitchen.

Carried rubbed her forehead. "I must apologize. I... don't know what came over me."

Cade stared at her for the longest time, making her uncomfortable. If he had something to say, she wished he'd just say it. She wasn't a mind reader.

"Perhaps Tilly is correct. I was too nervous to eat this morning."

His gaze narrowed. "Carrie? How long has it been since your husband died?"

She scrunched her forehead. What an odd question. "Approximately two months. Why?"

"Could it be possible that you're pregnant?"

Embarrassment swept over her, heating her face considerably. What was he suggesting, especially since he didn't want to be a doctor?

"I think, Mr. Hamilton, that is none of your business."

He arched an eyebrow. "So, you don't think you are pregnant?"

Panic welled inside her, and her mind scrambled to remember the last time she and Michael had been intimate. She quickly calculated the dates and then breathed a sigh of relief. "No, I'm not pregnant."

"Are you certain?"

Carrie wasn't about to tell Cade that she and Michael hadn't been intimate for several months, and it had nothing to do with her being tired because she was up with Parker Joe most of the night, either. Her heart wrenched. No, their lack of intimacy was not her fault.

Michael had somehow grown distant six months ago, and she'd never found the courage to ask him why.

She blinked back the tears threatening to spring forth. "Yes, I'm certain."

He rose to his feet and folded his arms, still staring at her with an expression of blame. "So, was that just an act?" He motioned his head toward the window. "Were you just pretending to faint in hopes that I would realize that I need to be a doctor?"

Anger flowed through her, making her headache worse. She sat up quickly, which made her dizzy, but she bit back the fog clouding her vision. "How dare you accuse me of doing that. Of course, it wasn't an act." She paused, and this time, she couldn't stop the words she'd wanted to say. "But if you had been a doctor, you would have seen that, wouldn't you? A good doctor would have known if someone was feigning their own sickness." She slowly stood, only to keep the dizziness from taking over again. "And a good doctor would have noticed that Tilly," she lowered her voice, pointing toward the kitchen, "is not well, either. And a good doctor would have wanted to treat her."

Cade's mouth tightened, and his hands bunched into fists. "Which is why I'm not a doctor," he bit out. "Because I'm not *good*, and I never will be." He turned and marched to the front door. "I'm going for a walk."

Oh! She wanted to scream, but then that would just make her headache worse. Instead, she moved into the kitchen to help Tilly. Her maid needed rest, and Carrie was going to make sure that Tilly's health improved, especially since she couldn't rely on the man she'd married.

"I'm well now," Carrie told Tilly as she moved beside her to take over. "You need to go lay down."

"I'm feeling fine, child." Tilly shooed Carrie away with her hands. "You need to be with your new husband."

Carrie groaned and rolled her eyes. "Oh, Tilly. I made such a mistake by picking him. I can't believe I went through with the marriage ceremony."

Tilly dropped the knife on the counter and turned to Carrie, taking hold of her hands. "Now listen to me. I know you're not ready to have a new husband, but you need to think of Parker Joe, too. Both of you *need* this man in your life. It will take some time to adjust, but you will, and so will Mr. Hamilton." Tilly squeezed Carrie's hands gently. "Be patient with him. Husbands do not come ready-made."

Carrie chuckled lightly. Tilly was famous for not beating around the bush. "You're right." Carrie sighed. "But Tilly, he doesn't want to be a doctor."

The older woman's forehead crinkled. "For heaven's sake, why not?"

"He won't tell me, but I need to change his mind somehow. This town needs a good doctor. *You* need a good doctor so that you can get well."

Tilly released Carrie's hands and hugged her. "Don't worry about me. My malady will soon be gone." The woman withdrew and peered into Carrie's eyes. "But you need to make your husband your priority. He came all the way out here to help you, knowing your situation and what has happened to our town. Now it's your turn to meet him halfway."

"Yes, Tilly. I shall try." Although the words came from Carrie's mouth, she doubted it would work.

* * * *

Cade stood in the barn, looking around at the pathetic and very sad scene. She had one goat and one chicken. His heart sank. He'd heard the conditions of this town were minimal, but he never suspected their livestock would be meager, as well.

Thankfully, he'd saved money from when he had been practicing medicine, and he would make sure they had some animals soon.

Slowly, he moved through the barn, taking a mental inventory of other things they needed as he let his anger cool. Carrie had no right to throw the blame on him for changing his mind about being a doctor. Women changed their minds all the time, and they never got ridiculed for doing it.

It was bad enough that Cade was fighting his own insecurities, he didn't need Carrie to say the words he'd been feeling for a while. He just wasn't good enough.

Releasing a pent-up breath, he ran his fingers through his hair. Apparently, his work as a farmer was cut out for him here in Last Chance. These women were going to need someone experienced in farming to help them with their crops and animals. Within a year, this town would be productive again.

He turned toward the goat's stall and tossed more hay on the ground. As Cade leaned against the wooden beam and watched the animal eat, his mind wandered back to Carrie and her harsh words. For the past few months, he'd been trying to overcome the guilt that had filled him when Clarence died.

The little boy had been an active five-year-old and smart as a whip. The boy's parents had been highly complimentary of the new doctor in town, and for a while, Cade thought he was invincible. He'd been warned not to let his popularity go to his head, but he couldn't stop it from happening.

Then, the fateful day came when little Clarence had received some kind of infectious disease. Both Cade and the other doctor couldn't figure out what it was or how to cure it. Cade researched day and night for nearly a week, not getting much sleep himself as he tried to find a cure for whatever the little boy had. His parents had continued to place their faith in God – and in Cade – but it wasn't enough, and the little boy died.

Doctor Dawson tried to convince Cade it wasn't his fault and that things like this happen, but when Cade had to see the blame on Clarence's family's face every time he saw them and hear the negative whispers about Cade's incompetence, the dejection was a hard pill to swallow.

Soon, people stopped making appointments to see Cade. He had continued to pray to God for some direction, but after a few months without his prayers being answered, Cade had given up hope. It wasn't long afterward when he'd read the article in the newspaper about Last Chance and the widows needing help. That was when he knew his purpose.

And he wouldn't let Carrie try to change his mind. He needed to do something to feel needed and important, or he'd just be a pathetic man struggling to find worth.

It wasn't until he heard a woman sigh when he realized he wasn't alone. He'd been so involved with his thoughts, he hadn't heard Carrie come in and lean against the half-wall of the stall. He tried to compose himself, not wanting to argue.

A few awkward seconds passed as she stared at the goat. Cade shifted from one foot to the other, not knowing how to start a conversation.

"We named the goat Snowflake," Carrie said. "And the chicken is Mrs. Cluckers."

He wanted to laugh but refrained. "You name your animals?"

Her gaze finally met his, and she nodded. "We had more a couple of months ago, but the blizzard brought freezing temperatures, and most of the town lost their livestock."

"I'm sorry you had to suffer through that terrible time," he said honestly. He really couldn't imagine how these women in town held up.

"Yes, well…" She took a deep breath and exhaled slowly. "I cannot dwell on the past. I must continue to move forward for my son."

"That's a wise choice."

She took another couple of breaths before she squared her shoulders, keeping her gaze on him. "I want to apologize for saying what I did." She shrugged. "There is no excuse, except for I've been nervous all day and expecting a doctor to be my husband, and when you told me you didn't want to, I well… I didn't handle it well."

He studied her expression, wondering if he could read her, but he couldn't. "Tell me, Carrie. Did you set out to marry a doctor? Knowing how you were raised, I'm now wondering if you were trying to find a husband who could make a hefty-size income."

Her jaw tightened, and her nostrils flared. Her chest rose and fell rapidly. Cade really hadn't set out to upset her, but he just needed to know if she was marrying him for his money.

"I realize we haven't seen each other since we were still in school, but I assure you, I'm not the type who marries for money as my mother had. I was in love with Michael when we married, and he was ambitious enough to go after his dream, which coincidentally, made pretty good money for a while. And, as I have mentioned a few times already, since his death, we haven't had the money for necessities. I'm surprised we haven't starved by now."

Cade nodded. "Forgive me for upsetting you, but I had to know."

Her shoulders relaxed slightly. "Cade, I wanted you to be a doctor because our town doesn't have one, and with Tilly ill, I wanted someone to care for her."

It was Cade's turn to stiffen, and he bunched his fingers into fists. "I'm sure it's just the common cold and that she'll recover soon."

"If you say so." Her gaze dropped back to the goat. "Will you tell me why you don't want to be a doctor?"

"No," he said quickly, wishing he hadn't. "I'm not ready to talk about it."

She stayed quiet for a few more minutes longer. The goat slowly munched on the hay and switched its gaze between Cade and the ground. He hoped the animal wouldn't give him any problems.

"Are you going to stay out here all day?" she asked. "I thought you could come inside and unpack your trunks."

The air between them just turned thicker. Either that or his chest was tightening. "Actually, I thought I'd sleep out here until—"

"No!" She gasped and jumped toward him, clinging to his arm. Her eyes were wide, and her face had paled slightly. "I won't have you so far from the house."

He narrowed his gaze. "Carrie, it's okay. I've slept in barns before."

"No, you don't understand." She inhaled shakily. "When the blizzard hit, it was so sudden, and the snow fell quickly. Some husbands were in the barn while their wives were in the house. Some of those men died, and the ones who didn't left days later to search for the hunting party and were killed anyway."

Her voice choked, and Cade's heart dropped. Now he understood her fear. It was on the tip of his tongue to tell her that he'd lived through bad snowstorms before, yet, he didn't want to make light of her situation.

Cade patted her hands, still clinging to his arm. "Then, I'll come inside."

A heavy sigh escaped her throat as color returned to her face. "Thank you. I appreciate it."

He turned with her as they slowly left the barn, retracing their steps toward the house. She walked closer to him this time, but she didn't touch him.

"Cade? I don't understand why you want to be a farmer over a doctor, but I'll try. However, will you do something for me?"

He was leery of answering, but he needed to know what kind of bargain she wanted to make. "What?"

"I'll let you show me why you want to be a farmer. However, in exchange, I would like for you to remember how to be a doctor."

He stopped and folded his arms. "Are you that worried about Tilly?"

She nodded as tears filled her eyes. "I can't lose her."

"Fine. I'll promise to tend to Tilly as long as you allow me to be a farmer."

A shaky smile touched her face. "Thank you."

Cade really hoped this wasn't the beginning of her trying to turn him back into a doctor. Only time would tell.

FOUR

Carrie's heart was racing as she prepared herself for bed that night. She had changed into her white cotton nightdress and slipped into her blue wrapper. Earlier, Cade had stocked wood in each room near the hearths to keep them warm during the night. As promised, he checked Tilly and told her to rest tomorrow. Carrie didn't see her maid doing that, but maybe with Cade in the house now, Tilly would do as he asked.

She had introduced Parker Joe to Cade, but her little one didn't want to get to know his new father. She knew it would take some time. Thankfully, Cade acted like he was interested in her son. She prayed Cade would turn out to be a good father, like Michael.

Taking a deep breath, she stared at her reflection through the mirror on her vanity table. Had she brushed her hair one-hundred times yet? She'd lost count when her thoughts took over. Perhaps she should brush it ten more times to be certain.

As she lifted the brush to her long hair, someone knocked on the bedroom door. Her breath stalled in her throat. *It's Cade!*

The moment she'd dreaded would soon be upon her. Although she knew it had to be done, it wasn't easy for her to accept.

"Come in," she said in a tight voice.

Without turning to look, she watched through the mirror as Cade opened the door and came inside. As soon as he saw her at the vanity, he stopped. His gaze moved over her hair and her nightclothes. His Adam's apple jumped in his throat. At least she wasn't the only one nervous about tonight.

"I... thought you'd be in bed by now." Cade closed the door, moved to the single chair near the window, and sat.

"No. It takes a while for me to calm down enough to rest." She set the brush on the vanity table and stood. Trying not to look at Cade, she stepped toward the bed and took off her wrapper. Her hands shook as she lowered the covers on the bed.

"You know, Carrie, if this is too uncomfortable for you, I can sleep on the couch or the floor in front of the hearth."

The thought had crossed her mind, but then she pushed it away. She needed to get used to her new marriage now, or she never would. "No, you don't have to do that. This bed is big enough for the two of us."

As she climbed onto the mattress, her thoughts briefly returned to Michael. There were many nights she went to bed alone because he was working late. Several times she'd gone to bed upset at him and slept closer to her side of the bed while he hugged his side of the bed all night. Indeed, the bed was large enough for two people who didn't want to touch each other while sleeping.

Carrie adjusted herself on the mattress and pulled the blankets up to her chin. She tried to avoid looking at Cade. There was something different about his expression tonight, which made her heart thump quicker. She was certain he was thinking about what would – or would not – happen tonight, too.

"Where should I undress?" he asked after a few seconds of nervous silence.

"Right where you're at is fine." Carrie rolled on her side, facing the opposite direction.

During the next few minutes, all she heard was his jeans' crackling and the rustling of fabric against fabric, and then his boots dropping to the floor. She squeezed her eyes closed, but that didn't make the sound disappear, and it definitely didn't help the images popping into her head. He was slightly taller than Michael, and Cade appeared to be built better, as well. She always thought Michael should eat more to put more meat on his bones.

The bed shifted as he climbed on the mattress, and then the covers tugged toward him. Carrie took a few deep breaths, trying to calm herself, but it wasn't working. She felt the tension between her and the man lying next to her, and she didn't know how to make it go away.

"Carrie," he finally said. "We don't need to do anything tonight, you know."

Relief weakened her limbs, yet at the same time, it also sped up her heartbeat. Cade *was* thinking about the same thing that had been on her mind.

"I…" she licked her dry lips as she opened her eyes and stared at the wall, "I just think it's too soon."

"So do I."

She expelled the gush of air still in her lungs. "I'm glad we agree on something."

Carrie watched the low light from the lamp dance on the wall. Although she'd rather be looking at him, she knew it wasn't a wise choice to make right now. She didn't want him to think she'd changed her mind. But she was wide awake, and she needed something to calm her down.

Her mind scrambled to think of a topic. All she knew about Cade was the rotten boy he used to be, his family, and especially his older brother, who she'd had a crush on. "So, tell me, Cade, how are your brother and sister doing?"

"They are all doing fine. My brother, Jacob, is a lumberjack in a small logging town in Montana, and he's doing quite well for himself."

"That's wonderful. Is Jacob married?" Carrie didn't know why she asked. It wasn't like she still had a girl's crush on him.

"No. He was engaged a few times, but he never married."

"Did he call off the wedding, or was it the woman?"

Cade chuckled. "He did. He claimed he wasn't ready."

"What about your sister, Savannah? Is she married yet?"

"No. The last time I spoke with Ma, she was getting desperate to find Savannah a husband. She's become quite the wild-child in New York."

"Oh, dear. That can't be good." She drew the tip of her finger over the patterns in the quilt. "Perhaps your parents should send her to where your brother is living. I'm sure the logging town has plenty of single men in need of a good wife."

A laugh came from Cade. "How do you know she'll make a *good* wife?"

"You are just awful." Carrie grinned and reached behind her to hit Cade. When her fingers brushed against his arm, she realized it was bare. Holding her breath, her heartbeat quickened once again. Was he one who liked to sleep in his *altogether*?

She gulped down a hard swallow, praying he wasn't like that. She definitely couldn't sleep with a man who didn't wear anything to bed.

"I'm sorry, you're right." Laughter was still in his voice. "I'm sure once my sister matures a little more, she'll make a… decent wife."

"I'm sure she will," she answered in a small voice. "And when that happens, your parents will be relieved."

"Actually, it's only my mother because…" Suddenly, his hand tenderly landed on her shoulder. "Carrie? I don't enjoy talking to the back of your head. Please turn and face me."

She didn't dare… Then again, she didn't want Cade to think she was frightened of a man's body – or *him* in general.

Taking a deep breath, she found the courage to turn in bed, keeping the covers over her the best she could. As soon as her gaze landed on Cade, she immediately noticed his bare arms folded behind his head and the top part of his bare chest that the quilt wasn't covering.

Oh, my! It was all she could do not to sigh aloud and let him know how much she admired his muscular body. Her body began trembling, and she tried not to let him see.

"Cade," she said in a scratchy voice that was entirely too deep. "Forgive me for asking, but do you usually sleep… this way… at night?"

"You mean without a shirt?"

Relief flooded her again. Thankfully, Cade was wearing something on the lower half of his body. "Yes, without a shirt."

He shrugged. "Usually."

"Won't you get cold?"

He shook his head. "Not generally."

"It gets really cold here in the winter."

He smiled. "Thanks for the warning."

She struggled to keep her gaze on his face, but occasionally, it drifted down to his bare and very *wide* shoulders. Michael wouldn't have liked Cade at all. Her husband never did like men when they showed off their muscles.

Carrie snapped her thoughts back to the conversation. "So, what were you saying about your parents? Are they still in New York?"

"Pa moved him and Ma to the big city because of her allergies. He became an accountant, but then about five years ago, he was hit by a runaway carriage and killed instantly."

Carrie gasped. "Oh, Cade. That's awful. I'm so sorry."

"It was a shock to the whole family. But Ma and Savannah are doing pretty well in Upstate, New York. Ma is a seamstress."

"I'm glad she can do that."

"And what about your parents?" Cade wondered. "Is your father still a lawyer?"

She nodded. "Not much has changed with them. My father is always helping a client, and Mother is usually out socializing."

"What did they think of you moving clear out here?"

"They didn't like it one bit, but Michael and I felt this was where we wanted to raise our children." Her voice broke as despair came over her. They had dreams, and now they were shattered.

"I'm sorry."

She inhaled a shaky breath. Crying now wouldn't solve anything. It would just make her more miserable. "Forgive me for bringing up the past. I shall try not to let it happen again."

"I understand you're still in mourning, Carrie. Please don't think you can't talk about the past because you can."

She struggled to smile. "But it wouldn't be right to think I'm comparing you with Michael. You and he are not alike in any way."

"Then, I won't be competing with his memory?" Cade asked.

She wanted to tell him, no, and yet, deep down in her heart, she knew he would be. Michael had been a good man. Cade would have to prove his worth, not only to her but also to Tilly and Parker Joe – and maybe even the rest of the town.

"Cade, I'm still mourning, but eventually, I'll realize Michael is not coming back."

He rolled to his side, facing her. She held her breath, not wanting him this close, and yet, the longer she gazed into his eyes, her heart began to soften. Perhaps her mourning period wouldn't be that much longer, and she could start to really like Cade Hamilton.

"I understand, Carrie." He touched her hand. "And I'm here to help you in *any* way."

The flutters in her chest increased. He was too darn charming and good-looking for his own good… It would be hard to resist this man, she just knew it.

FIVE

Cade couldn't sleep any longer. Usually, once the sun made its debut, he was out of bed and getting ready to start the day. However, when a woman's warm body was cuddled up next to him, it was near impossible to leave the comfort.

As his mind slowly came alert and he opened his eyes, he couldn't believe that Carrie was in his arms. He wasn't sure how that happened, but at the moment, he wasn't going to question fate – just enjoy the rewards of being a new husband… well, at least *some* of the rewards.

He realized Carrie was much prettier than she'd been as a little girl. Of course, he didn't expect her to stay the same, but she'd grown into a woman's body, and she now had real womanly issues to deal with. Laying in his arms like this, with her head resting in the crook of his shoulder and her hand positioned perfectly over his heart, she appeared so peaceful. With her long eyelashes, and her tempting heart-shaped mouth, and the loose dark hair curling down over her shoulders, she looked desirous.

Cade shouldn't be having thoughts like this. He'd realized last night that he might never measure up to her precious Michael. Cade would probably always be the fill-in husband. Yet, there was a moment during their conversation last night before they fell asleep, which made him hope for a happier future. Their marriage had started badly, but with a lot of work from both of them, he was sure they could eventually fall in love.

Expelling a breath, he very slowly started pulling away from her. The movement jarred her momentarily awake because she moaned and slid her arm around his waist, holding onto him. He gritted his teeth. Why had she done that? If only she knew it was him, she held onto and not her precious Michael...

Once her breathing became regular again, he tried once more to leave her side. Carefully, he lifted her arm from around his waist as he slowly moved away. Just when he thought he could break free this time, she let out another moan, and her whole body snuggled beside him. Her leg even hooked across his leg. This was not good!

Yet, it felt nice. Too nice. If he didn't find some way to move away from her now, he'd be in big trouble. Lonely men like himself were weak when it came to enticingly beautiful women like Carrie.

Although his mind kept telling him she was his wife, he knew he must give her the time needed to adjust to him. He couldn't start kissing her unless she welcomed it.

Finally, he was able to pull away. When she blindly reached for him, he snatched his pillow and put it under her hand. She took it and pressed it against her bosom as she continued to sleep.

Sighing with relief, he didn't waste time as he readied himself for the day. Just as he slid on his boots, he heard Parker Joe crying from down the hallway. Cade's attention snapped to Carrie, thinking she would wake up, but she continued to sleep like an unconscious person.

He left the bedroom and walked down the hallway toward the baby's room. He opened the door and peeked inside. The room was still slightly warm with a small fire still burning in the hearth, which meant Tilly must have checked on the baby sometime during the night. Parker Joe sat in his crib, and when the baby saw Cade, his crying stopped immediately. The baby's eyes widened in fear. Cade didn't want to scare the poor kid, and yet, it appeared the women in the house weren't waking up to help Parker Joe.

Cade stepped out of the room and moved to Tilly's room. Her door was ajar, so he slowly pushed it open. "Tilly?" When he heard no answer, he opened the door wider. The older woman was in bed, but her room wasn't as warm as the baby's. There was also a distinct odor – one that he would always remember. It was the scent of sickness.

Inwardly, he groaned. He needed to bring Doctor Hamilton out of retirement long enough to get Carrie's maid feeling better.

Cade hurried to her bed and placed his hand on her sweaty brow. The woman was burning up.

Cussing under his breath, he spun around and ran to Carrie's bedroom. He rushed inside and to the bed. "Carrie, wake up. Tilly needs your help."

Groggily, Carrie blinked open her eyes. Dazed and clearly confused, she looked around the room before her gaze snapped back to him.

"Carrie, Parker Joe is crying, but Tilly cannot mind the baby. She has a very high fever, and I—"

Quick as lightning, Carrie jumped out of bed. As she slipped on her wrapper, she stepped into her slippers. Cade moved down the hall, leading the way. Carrie rushed past him to Tilly's side.

"Tilly? Can you hear me?" Carrie gently touched the woman's forehead. Tears formed in Carrie's eyes, and as the seconds turned into minutes and Tilly still hadn't awakened, Carrie's tears slid down her cheeks in gushes. "Cade? Can you… help her?"

He nodded. "I'll try my hardest. But you need to take care of your son first. Let me take care of Tilly."

Nodding, she wiped the tears from her eyes. "Thank you, Cade."

He waited for Carrie to leave the room before he checked the older woman more thoroughly. He had to retrieve his stethoscope and tongue compressor from his medical bag in one of his trunks, but he was able to listen to Tilly's breathing. She had fluid in her lungs. *Pneumonia.*

Her fever was high, and he needed to bring it down quickly. Not often was he grateful for lots of snow, but this would be one of the rare moments. He hurried outside to the barn and found an empty bucket, and then hurried to the snow-packed ground and scooped several handfuls of snow into the bucket.

Once inside Tilly's room, he packed the snow around her neck and head, and then in her armpits and even between her legs. He'd only treated one case of pneumonia, and the woman wasn't this bad off. But he had watched Doctor Dawson with a very ill patient with a high fever, and this was what the doctor had done.

Cade prayed he could still save her and that he would remember how not to panic.

* * * *

Carrie had gotten her fussy baby to sleep again, and as she rocked him in the rocking chair, she listened intently for any sounds of Tilly waking up. Cade had been in and out of the maid's room for two hours, and as time passed slowly, her fears escalated. She couldn't lose Tilly. It had been devastating enough to lose her husband, but Tilly… she was like an aunt to Carrie. That woman had been part of Carrie's heart for so long, she didn't think she'd be able to handle having the woman die.

"Please, Lord," Carrie whispered brokenly, "don't take Tilly from me."

It surprised her that she still had tears to shed since she thought she had used them all up when Michael died. But her tears wouldn't stop, not until Cade gave her some good news.

During the wait, her mind replayed the strange dream she had last night. She'd felt as if she was in a man's strong arms, with her hand on his bare chest… and she *liked* it. The man in her dream couldn't have possibly been Michael, because he always wore a nightshirt. What bothered her more than anything were the tingling feelings she'd received during this dream and knowing it wasn't about Michael.

When Cade had snapped her awake, and as she rushed in to check on Tilly, her body had still felt as though she was in his arms. It was a most disturbing feeling, yet… a very curious sensation that made her want to experience it again.

After what seemed like forever, the floor squeaked as Cade stepped into the nursery. His hair was tousled, his shirt was opened wide at his throat, and his sleeves were rolled up to his elbows, but she didn't think she would ever see another man look so handsome as he did. Relief was on his expression, and he gave her a tired smile.

"Her fever has broken," he said softly.

Tears of happiness welled in Carrie's eyes. She wanted to shout in joy, but waking little Parker Joe wasn't a good idea. "Is she awake?"

He nodded. "After the fever broke, she opened her eyes and thanked me."

"Will she recover?"

He inhaled a shaky breath. "I pray she will. She has pneumonia, and it's hard for her to breathe. She will need to cough out the infection from her body. I hope she's strong enough."

"She has always been strong." After Carrie said it, she thought back on her life and realized that Tilly didn't get sick very often. Hopefully, that would mean she was a fighter.

Cade softly stepped into the room, moving closer to Carrie. His gaze dropped to little Parker Joe. "How is your son?"

Carrie's heart melted that he would think of the baby at this time. "He's fine."

"He hasn't gotten sick?"

She shook her head. "And I pray he doesn't."

"I wouldn't wish that on anyone." He lifted his hand and touched her cheek in a light caress. "How are you holding up?"

She wasn't sure she liked – or understood – the butterflies dancing in her belly right now or the way his gaze made her warm inside. Neither did she like that the feelings she'd had in her dreams were back. Then again, maybe she did like it after all. "I've had worse days."

"I'm sure you have." He motioned toward the kitchen. "I'll make soup for lunch. That'll be better for Tilly's body, anyway."

"I'll lay Parker Joe down and come help you."

Carrie struggled to stand with the baby in her arms, so Cade assisted. His hands on her arms felt oddly comforting. He also helped lay her son in his crib. Having Cade this close to her was doing crazy little things to her body, making her limbs quake.

She wasn't certain why she told him she'd help. Tilly had always made the meals. All Carrie helped with was peeling the potatoes and carrots or chopping the onions. But Cade would find out soon enough what kind of a wife she'd been to Michael, so it might as well be today.

They didn't speak as they left the nursery and walked to the kitchen. Her nerves were jumping like hot kernels, and her heartbeat whacked against her ribs so hard she thought it would leave bruises. Her mind pictured him as he'd been in her dreams last night, which only made her emotions go insane.

"Do you mind if I just snoop through your kitchen?" he asked.

"Go right ahead." Carrie moved to the closet where Tilly kept the vegetables. "What type of soup should we make?"

"Chicken broth?"

"How about bone broth with vegetables? I fear we are limited down to one chicken for eggs."

"Then bone broth with vegetables sounds delicious."

She mentally patted herself on the back for at least acting like she knew what she was doing. As she and Cade peeled potatoes, she struggled to remember the times she'd helped Tilly make the soup. She must remember every step, even down to adding the spices.

"Carrie?" Cade asked without looking up from the potato he was peeling. "Why did you name your son Parker Joe? I'd thought your husband would have wanted Michael junior."

"I suggested that to Michael, but he was adamant about Parker Joe. All he told me was that he had a childhood friend named Parker Joe, and Michael wanted to name his first-born child after his friend." She paused, staring at Cade. "Why would you ask?"

"This will sound strange, but I knew a woman with that name."

She scrunched her forehead. "You knew a woman with a man's name?"

"She spelled her middle name J.O."

"Oh, I see." Carrie shrugged. "I suppose it's a common name."

Cade paused, looking at her. "But it's not. Parker, yes, and Jo – short for Josephine – yes, but the two names combined as though you're saying one name? That's not common at all."

As Carrie thought back to all of the people she'd met over the years, she realized Cade was correct. "Well, then I suppose it is strange that you would know a woman by that name." She paused briefly. "Where did you know her?"

"She worked at Bellevue hospital, where I was an intern. That would have been almost four years ago."

A chill passed through Carrie, and she couldn't move her hands to continue peeling. Her mind buzzed with memories of what Michael had told her about when his mother was in Bellevue's hospital for a month. That had happened right before Michael started courting Carrie.

What were the odds that the Parker Joe Michael spoke of was the same Parker Jo that Cade referred to?

She cleared her throat that was suddenly clogging with the bile from her churning stomach. "What did this lady look like?"

Cade glanced back at her, and for a brief moment, his gaze swept over her face and hair. "She has long brown hair as you do. Her face is more round, and her cheeks are pudgy."

"She was a fat woman?"

Cade chuckled. "No, it's just that her face was round, which made her cheeks bigger."

"How old was she?"

"She is probably around your age." He returned to peeling his potato.

Carrie stared at the knife in her hand, not seeing what she was doing. Her spinning thoughts wouldn't allow her to concentrate on anything else. Michael had talked about his friend, taking long walks with him, riding horses through the countryside, and even having snowball fights with some of the others their age. When Michael spoke of his friend, his eyes lit up, and his cheeks turned pink. It was as if Michael had drifted away to another place and time to relive his happiest moments.

Other memories filled Carrie's head. When she was heavy with child, Michael had gone into a deep melancholy. At the time, she had thought he was just nervous about being a father, just as she was anxious about being a mother. One particular night, he'd drank a little too much whiskey, and during the night, he'd rolled over to hold her and whispered *Parker*. At the time, she wasn't sure about the second name he'd muttered. The next morning when she'd asked him about it, he said he'd been dreaming of his childhood friend, Parker Joe, and he wanted to give their child that name. She had agreed, but if the baby was a girl, she had wanted to name it.

Carrie's stomach lurched, and she gnashed her teeth, trying not to lose what little was in her stomach. Michael had been in love with a woman whom his parents didn't approve of, which was why he had started courting Carrie. He'd told her many times over the years how grateful he was for marrying her and not the other woman. Yet, if this other woman was Parker Jo… Had he been thinking about her the whole time he'd been married to Carrie?

As though in a tunnel, she heard her name being called – softly at first, before growing louder and louder. As she snapped back to reality, Cade was kneeling in front of her, holding her hands. His expression was one of worry. On the table was the knife and potato... what was left of the potato after she had nearly massacred it.

"Carrie? Can you hear me now?"

Her breaths had become irregular, and her body trembled violently. "I... I can hear you."

"What just happened?" He released her hands and cupped her face. "Carrie, you were stabbing your knife into the potato so viciously that I thought you might injure yourself."

She wanted to laugh it off, embarrassed about being caught acting like a madwoman, but she didn't have the energy for humor right now. "I... I need some air. I need... to be alone."

Pushing away from Cade, she hurried outside, not caring that she didn't have her jacket or cloak to ward off the chill in the air. However, she knew the coolness against her hot face would bring some relief to the rage rolling through her. Sadly, she doubted it would help the memories disappear.

SIX

Cade wasn't sure how to act. Dealing with his sister's emotional days was nothing like what Carrie was going through. Then again, he hadn't cared to help Savannah. That was his mother's problem, not his. But Carrie was his problem now... and he really wanted to help her.

Before hurrying outside, she'd told him she wanted to be alone. But as he watched her out the window, he noticed the turmoil in her expression as she walked aimlessly around the yard. Being a doctor, he didn't want her out in the cold without warm boots and a warm cloak, but he also didn't want to upset her by asking her to come inside.

Sometime during the morning, as he was caring for Tilly, Carrie had dressed for the day, wearing a lovely lavender blouse with a black skirt. She had pulled her hair back and tied it with a black ribbon. He liked that she didn't wear her hair like most married women – coiled so tight at the back of their head that their eyes nearly popped out. He enjoyed seeing her hair long and flowing over her shoulders and down her back... just as she'd been this morning while curled up in his arms.

Cade wasn't sure what had made her this way. They'd been talking about how her son had gotten his name. And once Carrie asked what Parker Jo looked like, Carrie's mind had just taken off to a different place. He had watched her closely, realizing that she wasn't paying attention to him or peeling the potato, but when she started stabbing the vegetable as her brown eyes clouded over with tears of anger, he knew it was time to take the knife out of her hand.

When he had called out to her a few times, and she hadn't heard him, he feared she'd gone mad. Now he worried that this was a common thing for her to do. Dear heavens, he hoped not, but it made sense why her parents allowed her to take the family maid with her once she married and moved away from home.

Or maybe... Carrie was just a troubled woman, still trying to recover from her mourning period. He wanted to believe that second option.

Cade noticed her heavy cloak hanging on the peg next to the door. He grabbed the garment and hurried outside. Carrie didn't notice him until he was almost right next to her. She jumped, and her brown eyes grew wide. He didn't say anything but held up her cloak in a silent offering to help.

As she stared at him, tears swam in her eyes, and she stepped into the garment while he wrapped it around her shoulders. Within seconds, her body shook as sobs of anguish came from her throat. Immediately, she turned toward him and pressed her face against his chest.

Hearing her heart-wrenching sobs nearly tore him apart. He circled his arms around her, pulling her closer to him. He pressed his mouth against her head, giving her a tender kiss of reassurance.

Cade wished she would talk to him, and although she might not be ready, he hoped that she would soon open up. How else would he be able to say the right comforting words to her?

After a few minutes, her crying subsided. She stayed in his arms as he rubbed her back. Her breaths were ragged, but at least she wasn't sobbing uncontrollably. Heaving another breath, she tilted her head back and looked up at him.

He offered a sweet smile and gently stroked her moist cheeks, removing the tears. "Do you want to go inside?"

She nodded. "We need to get that soup made for Tilly."

"Yes, we do."

Keeping his arm around her shoulders, he turned them toward the house. It surprised him that she didn't pull away but walked with him inside. He removed her cloak and hung it back on the peg. She waited beside him, and then they went into the kitchen in silence and sat at the table. He picked up the knife she'd been using and looked at her with an arched eyebrow.

"Do I trust you to use this knife the right way now?"

She chuckled and nodded. "Yes, I'm fine. The person I would use this on is already dead, so you don't need to worry about me."

Confusion filled him. Was Carrie upset at Michael? It must have something to do with the woman Cade had mentioned.

"Do you want to talk about it?" he asked.

She stared at the knife as she blinked back tears. "Let's just say I realized something about Michael that I should have known before, but I was too blind to see." She inhaled deeply and straightened her shoulders. "And from this point forward, my son's name will be PJ."

Cade nodded. "I understand."

Carrie took another potato and started peeling. "Will you tell me about some experiences you had as a doctor? I need something to distract me from my depressing thoughts."

Although he didn't want to discuss those days as a doctor, he would help her out. He searched through his memory and found a humorous one. "When I first started working with Doctor Dawson, I met Mrs. Langely. She was an older woman who had every disorder in the book." Carrie's gaze snapped up, and her eyes widened. He chuckled. "So, the woman thought," he quickly explained. "There are some people who believe they are sick, and so, they are."

A small smile touched her face. "I had an aunt like that once."

"Then, you know how they complain about everything, and they are never satisfied."

"Never." She laughed.

"Well, Mrs. Langely started coming to see me because Doctor Dawson was tired of telling the woman she wasn't sick." He grinned, holding in a laugh. "I decided the best way to help this lady was to lie to her."

"Lie?" Carrie gasped. "Why would you do that?"

"I told her," Cade continued without answering her question, knowing the story itself would be the answer, "that she had one year to live. She believed she had bad lungs because she coughed all the time." He shrugged. "Her husband smoked a pipe all the time, and I'm sure her breathing problems came from that. Anyway, I told her that she had one year to live, so she needed to make the best of those twelve months. She needed to be loving and kind to everyone, reminding her what the Bible says about how we will be judged for our good deeds."

Carrie sucked in a quick breath and slapped a hand over her mouth. Laughter twinkled in her pretty brown eyes.

"For three months straight, Mrs. Langely did as I requested. Her family and friends thought she was a changed woman. Mrs. Langely didn't visit the hospital as much, and when she did come in, it was to bring us a cake she'd made or flowers that she had picked."

"Did she ever find out you had lied to her?" Carrie asked in a sweet voice.

"No." He chuckled softly. "I had quit being a doctor at that point, but before I left to come here, I rode past her, and she was out helping her invalid neighbor."

Carrie laughed. "I want to tell you how horrible you were for lying to her, but yet, that was probably the best diagnosis that anyone could have given her."

Cade's heart lightened from her words. "You think so?"

She nodded. "You made her stop thinking about herself and start thinking of others."

Cade left the table to find a large pot to put the vegetables in. "I'm glad you approve."

The chair's legs scraped the floor right before he heard Carrie's heeled boots move across the floor, coming toward him. He figured her hands would be full of the vegetables they had peeled, so he turned to take them from her, holding his hands out. Instead, she stepped right into his arms and rested her head against his chest. The suddenness of her actions had him holding his breath to see what she was going to do next.

"Thank you," she whispered brokenly.

His heart tugged as he wrapped his arms around her. "For what?"

"For thinking of me when I was outside and bringing me warmth from the cold." She tilted her head and met his gaze. "It's hard to admit, but I'm not used to a husband who thinks about others in that way."

Surprise washed over him. *Michael was selfish?* That concept was difficult to believe, but it made sense as to why Carrie had acted so shocked to see him bringing her the garment.

Cade caressed her cheek. "I'm sorry you're not used to that. I'll make sure you won't have to say that about your current husband."

She smiled softly. "And I promise that you will never have to say that about your wife, either."

Her gaze dropped to his mouth. This time, it was his turn to hitch his breath. Those feelings he'd experienced this morning after waking up holding this beautiful woman returned in full force. Did she want to be kissed? Yet, she'd gone through several different emotions today already, and he didn't think he should introduce his passionate side to her. Not today. They needed more time to get to know each other.

Although… giving her a little kiss would certainly help the process of becoming closer.

Silently, he scolded himself for having such thoughts. Rushing into this relationship was not a good idea.

Thankfully, PJ picked that moment to start fussing. It was all Cade could do not to sigh in relief. He was certain that if the baby hadn't interrupted them, Cade would have found another reason that kissing his new wife was a good idea.

Carrie stepped out of his arms, giving him a bashful smile before she turned and walked out of the kitchen. Cade released a heavy breath as he pushed his fingers through his hair. Perhaps it was too soon to touch her. However, she didn't seem to have a problem taking the first initiative to move into his arms.

She'd been through too much for Cade to do something stupid and ruin the growing friendship between them. He would have to take things one day at a time and let her make the first move if she wanted to kiss him.

SEVEN

After three more days, Tilly was finally out of bed and slowly walking around. It did Carrie's heart good to see the woman acting somewhat normal. Of course, Carrie made sure Tilly followed Cade's instructions to rest as much as possible. A few times, Tilly sat at the kitchen table and instructed Carrie on preparing a meal. It surprised her how quickly she understood how to cook, and so far, she hadn't burned anything.

Today was laundry day, and so Tilly watched little PJ so that Carrie could wash clothes. Thankfully, Tilly had instructed her how to do this wifely task and not shrink any clothes. However, as she stood outside, hanging clothes on the line, her new husband distracted her in the worst way.

The weather seemed slightly warmer today – either that or she was over-heated because of watching him work around the yard. He had been repairing fences the past two days, and she found enjoyment in watching the way his shirt practically clung to his muscular chest and arms as he swung the ax to cut the wood. She also found herself peeking at him much too often when he bent over to nail the slabs of wood into the posts, admiring the way his trousers fit snuggly against his legs.

She should be ashamed of herself... but then quickly remembered that he was her husband. She could ogle him all she wanted now without feeling guilty.

From the corner of her eye, a movement from the street caught her attention. Walking toward the house was

Miss Rebecca Sterling. The oldest daughter of seven children, Rebecca was now tasked with helping raise her brothers and sisters as her widowed mother had to take over the position at the bank where their father had worked before the freezing blizzard temperatures took his life. The blizzard also claimed Rebecca's fiancé as well.

Carrie quickly hung the wet garment on the line that was still in her hands before turning to meet Rebecca halfway. The young woman wore dark colors, showing that she was in mourning, but Carrie knew the lighter colors complimented Rebecca's complexion and brown hair. Hopefully, the young woman would return to her normal life soon.

"Good afternoon," Carrie greeted when Rebecca drew closer. She could tell by the forlorn expression on her friend's face that the visit wouldn't be very cheerful.

"Hello, Carrie." Rebecca gave Carrie a quick hug and pulled away. "I heard you were married the other day."

Carrie nodded and motioned toward Cade, who was now in an upright position, looking toward them as he wiped his moist brow.

Rebecca's smile widened slightly. "He's a fine man, for sure." She squeezed Carrie's hand gently. "I'm so happy you could find someone to help you."

"Yes, I was lucky to find him." Carrie glanced toward Cade again. He had turned back to fixing the fence, and her heart skipped a beat. "As fate would have it, Mr. Hamilton and I knew each other when we were children."

"How remarkable."

Carrie turned back toward her friend. "How is your mother doing? Is she trying to find a new husband?"

Rebecca's smile left her face. "No. Ma thinks she's too old."

Carrie's heart broke for Mrs. Sterling. Hooking her arm with Rebecca's, Carrie proceeded toward the house. "Come inside, and let's make some hot tea. It's still rather nippy out here to stand around and chat."

When they entered the house, Rebecca moved toward PJ, who played with toys on the floor. Tilly sat in the cushioned chair near the hearth, keeping an eye on the boy. She reached down and picked up PJ, hugging him and kissing him on the forehead. Rebecca greeted Tilly, as well.

"Tilly," Carrie said, stepping toward the kitchen. "I'm going to make some tea. Would you like some?"

"Yes, thank you, dear," the older woman said before coughing.

Rebecca set PJ back on the floor and then followed Carrie into the kitchen. Carrie placed the kettle of water on the hot stove before finding some teacups.

She joined Rebecca at the table as they waited for the water to boil. "What is your mother going to do?" Carrie frowned. "Pastor Collins is adamant about every widow finding a new husband to help them out on the prairie."

"Yes, Ma knows. She's exchanged heated words with the pastor about it, too. Ma realizes we can't live here any longer, and thankfully, her brother has wired us some money to help us move out west."

Carrie's heart dropped. "Move?" Her throat choked with emotion. "Oh, Rebecca, I don't want you to move."

Rebecca's eyes watered. "I don't want to go, either, but I cannot stay here by myself. Ma needs my help with my brothers and sisters."

"Where will you go?"

"Uncle Jack lives in a small place in Montana called Stumptown. He assured Ma that there would be many places to work in this logging town."

Carrie reached across the table and grasped Rebecca's hand. The young woman was of age to marry, and staying in Last Chance definitely wouldn't help her out in that regard. "I pray your uncle is correct. Your family needs to be happy."

Rebecca nodded. "I'll miss you greatly."

"And I, you."

"Ma mentioned there would be someone coming to run the bank soon, which is a relief. She doesn't have the money smarts to run a bank, not like Mr. Porter used to do."

Carrie's breath froze upon hearing Michael's name. "Yes, well... it takes someone with a head for business and making more money."

"Indeed, it does." Rebecca paused, and then surprise registered on her face. "Oh, I almost forgot. Ma wants you to come to the bank. She found something of Mr. Porter's that she thinks you'd like to have."

Carrie's stomach knotted. "What is it?"

"Ma didn't tell me what she found, just that I should have you come to the bank at your earliest convenience."

Although Carrie didn't want to see what Mrs. Sterling had found, she also wanted to put Michael in the past where he belonged. "I'll make sure to visit her tomorrow." She left the table to check on the water. Thankfully, it was almost ready for tea. As she prepared their drinks, her gut twisted with indecision. Was she wrong to judge Michael so harshly? And yet, he was the one who'd lied to her during their marriage. Did he think she would never find out? In ways, she wished she hadn't. It was easier to live in her dream world without knowing the truth.

She took Tilly her drink before returning to the kitchen and sitting at the table again. "Do you need any help packing?"

"No. I have enough brothers and sisters that can pack."

Sighing, Carrie lifted her teacup to her mouth and blew on the hot liquid before taking a sip. "Is there anything you need Mr. Hamilton or me to help your family with?"

Rebecca took a small drink and shrugged. "I suppose we need some help getting our wagon repaired enough to take us to the train station."

"I'll ask him if he has knowledge of that." Carrie smiled, figuring she already knew the answer. She was certain Cade knew about fixing wagons.

"We would appreciate it."

After taking another drink of her tea, Carrie reached across the table and grasped Rebecca's hand. "Oh, I'm going to miss you so much. You must promise to write letters. I want to know everything that happens in your life. I'm sure you'll meet the perfect man and fall madly in love."

Rebecca laughed. "Don't get your hopes up about that last part, but I promise to write to you."

The back door opened, and Cade walked inside, holding a bloody arm. Carrie gasped and jumped up to help. "Oh, dear. What happened?" She grabbed a dishcloth and handed it to him.

"I scratched my arm on a nail. It's nothing to worry about."

"Sit down." She pointed to her empty chair. "Let me get some bandages."

"Carrie, really – it's no trouble."

"Cade, sit," she commanded in a motherly tone. He looked surprised, but he did as she instructed. "If you'll excuse me," she told Rebecca, "but I need to tend to my husband."

"Of course, you do, and I'll leave you to it. I've got to go, but I'll talk to you when you go to the bank." She hurried out the door before Carrie could stop her.

But she wasn't going to stop Rebecca because right now, her husband's injury came first. She rushed to the supply of bandages she kept in the hall cupboard, and after grabbing a handful, returned to the kitchen. Cade was dabbing the dishcloth to his arm, wiping up the blood.

"Here, let me look at that." She took hold of his arm and lifted it slightly toward the window to have the sunlight to help her see it better. As she pulled the dishcloth out of his hand, her fingers grazed by his. Invisible sparks of energy grew between them. She held her breath and glanced at his face. His expression was as surprised as she felt. He must have felt it, too. Of course, knowing this made her heartbeat quicken.

She breathed through the sensations running through her chest and concentrated on his injury. Once she had removed the blood, she could see the depth of the cut… which wasn't deep at all.

Carrie lifted her gaze and met his. She arched an eyebrow. "You lost all that blood from *this*?"

He laughed. "I tried to tell you it was nothing."

The panic in her disappeared and was replaced by humor. Laughing, she playfully swatted Cade's shoulder. "You were bleeding all over. What was I supposed to think?"

He slid his other arm around her waist, pulling her closer to him. Suddenly, the light moment turned into sparks again. His green eyes turned darker as his expression relaxed, and his gaze dropped to her mouth.

"Thank you for caring about me and wanting to help me," he said in a soft voice.

Heavens, why had the rhythm of her heart accelerated? It surprised her how easily Cade affected her. She didn't want to think it was because she was a lonely widow. But strangely enough, she didn't think of herself as a widow any longer.

Was it too soon to give in to temptation and become a *real* wife to her new husband?

EIGHT

Carrie was curious. It was written all over her face. However, the longer Cade waited for her to make the first move, the intense energy between them was fizzling out. They were now entering the awkward moments, and one of them was going to have to pull away. Since she still looked undecided, the task was left up to him.

Clearing his throat, he dropped his arm from around her waist and glanced back at his scratch. Why he'd bled so much, he didn't know, but it appeared to have stopped. Then again, being a doctor, he also knew that he should keep his arm above his heart for a little while to give the inside of the wound time to heal.

"I didn't mean to make your friend run off." He took the dishcloth and finished wiping away the blood around the wound.

Carrie stepped away from him and proceeded to prepare a small bandage for his arm. "You didn't. She's a little shy around men, especially when they are so handsome…" She hitched a breath, and her eyes grew wide. Bright spots of red formed on her cheeks.

He chuckled over her blunder. "So, you think I'm handsome, huh?"

Carrie rolled her eyes. "Oh, Mr. Hamilton, I think you know that answer." She met his gaze. "You've always been handsome, and you flaunted it many times in school."

Cade shrugged. "Can I help it that the girls liked me?"

She shook her head. "If you recall, not *all* the girls liked you." She placed the gauze on his scratch and started to bind it with the bandage.

"I think you were the only one who didn't."

"That's because you pulled my pigtails all the time."

He grinned, remembering those days. "Maybe it's because I thought you were the prettiest girl in school."

She laughed harshly. "If you thought that way, you wouldn't have been torturing me."

"Torture?"

"Yes." She stopped and looked at him again. There was no laughter this time in her big brown eyes. "I had a tender head." She frowned. "I had pleaded with you to stop, but you never did."

His heart wrenched, seeing the pain of the past in her eyes. He needed to fix it now. "I'm sorry, Carrie. The truth is, I didn't stop because at least you paid some attention to a farmer's boy like I was." He tenderly touched her hand. "You were the rich girl in class, and I was the poor boy."

Slowly, her frown turned into a smile. "Really? It wasn't because you hated me?"

He shook his head. "Not at first. I had wanted your attention, which I'll admit, I went about it the wrong way. Then, after a while, when I could see it irritated you, I was upset because I didn't get the kind of reaction I'd wanted." He gently took hold of her hand and caressed her fingers. "Will you forgive me for being such a foolish dolt?"

She chuckled. "I think we were both foolish at that age, but yes, I forgive you."

He sighed in relief. At least that was over and done with. "Good, now…" He stood, hoping to get back to repairing the fence soon, but he tripped on the leg of the chair and stumbled into Carrie. She gasped and splayed her hands on his chest as he quickly balanced himself before they both toppled to the floor.

Immediately, his arms wrapped around her – an instinct to keep her from falling, he tried to tell himself. However, he realized he liked her this way. He enjoyed the way his heartbeat quickened and how he became breathless when they were this close.

Once more, the spark between them ignited, and this time, it was hotter than before. Carrie's attention moved to his mouth, and his throat became parched. He tried resisting the urge to kiss her, reminding himself that he wanted her to make the first move, but then a thought struck him upside of the head like a two-by-four wooden board. What if this was her way of making the first move? If that was the case, he couldn't possibly turn her down.

Slowly, he lowered his mouth. Her eyelids closed as she tilted back her head. This was definitely her making the first move.

He gently brushed his lips over hers, not wanting to startle her in any way. But, as he tried to take the kiss slowly, she rose up and wrapped her arms around his neck. The movement brought them closer, and he'd forgotten all about taking his time with their first passionate kiss.

Cade tightened her in his arms, tilting his head and deepening the kiss. She sucked in a quick breath, mere seconds before she sighed heavily. Her body relaxed against him, and he was sure that if he weren't holding her this way, she would have fallen to the ground.

In all the times he'd kissed a woman, they had never acted this way – as if kissing him made them melt. Knowing what he must be doing to her caused his own limbs to weaken and his heart to soar. He didn't want to stop kissing her now.

From the other room, Tilly started coughing uncontrollably. Cade could tell the older woman's chest was rattling by the way she wheezed. Carrie broke the kiss and stepped back. Her cheeks were pink, and her lips swollen, but it was her eyes that had him hypnotized. They were so dreamy.

Her chest rose and fell quickly. She shook her head. "I wish that blasted infection would leave Tilly's body once and for all."

"Give it time."

"I'd better go check on her."

He nodded. "And I should go back outside and finish repairing the fence."

She smiled almost bashfully and turned to head into the other room. Cade smiled. He liked how caring she was toward Tilly and that she treated the maid like family. Perhaps there was a huge heart in Carrie after all because the woman definitely knew how to be passionate.

* * * *

Carrie had wanted to see what would happen when she and Cade retired for bed that night, but she didn't dare. Besides, Tilly's coughing sounded so terrible, and Carrie's maid needed her help tonight. Cade had understood when she apologized for wanting to stay up and help Tilly. Of course, during the night, she also took care of her son, who was having a fitful night.

Dozing off and on during the night didn't give her much rest, and when the sun rose in the morning, she wasn't certain she would be able to make it through the day without dropping from exhaustion.

It surprised her when Cade woke up and made breakfast for all of them. Smelling the eggs cooking on the stove made her stomach grumble. She stood from the cushioned chair in Tilly's room and walked over to the bed on weary legs. The older woman was asleep, and thankfully, hadn't coughed for at least an hour.

Quietly, she left the room and closed the door. The voices coming from the kitchen couldn't possibly be what she was hearing. Then again, she was very tired and was probably dreaming this whole thing. But as she walked into the kitchen, Cade sat on the chair, holding PJ on his lap, as he fed him the scrambled eggs on his plate.

Her husband must not have noticed her because his focus was on her son. Cade's funny little sounds when he shoveled a spoonful of eggs and steered it to the baby's mouth were quite comical. Whatever Cade said, he wasn't very loud, but his tone of voice was playful and childish.

What surprised her even more was that PJ laughed at Cade… and ate the food. Apparently, her son was like every other male she knew – that food always made them happy.

She leaned her shoulder against the doorframe, mainly because she was tired, but she also wanted to watch without being seen. At least for a few minutes.

As her mind finally started coming alert, she realized that Michael had never done this with PJ. Michael had held their son and played with him a little, but he had never wanted to help her with the baby. Michael never offered to help feed PJ, either. Could she be witnessing what a good father does with his son?

Her eyes clouded over with happy tears, knowing for certain that PJ was going to have a good relationship with his new father and that Cade was going to be a loving father.

Carrie quickly wiped her eyes before Cade noticed. She didn't want to have to tell him why she was crying this time. It seemed she'd done it too much already... especially when her dead husband didn't deserve her tears and heartache.

PJ was the first to see her. He giggled and held out his hands toward her. Smiling, she pulled away from the doorframe and walked closer. Cade's gaze jumped up and met hers. He appeared almost embarrassed to be caught feeding the baby.

"I see you and PJ are getting along splendidly." She stopped beside Cade and took one of PJ's outstretched hands, but she didn't pick him up.

"Yes." Cade smiled down at the boy. "I'm relieved that he allowed me to feed him."

"I'm happy to see he's eating the eggs. He's never had that before."

Cade winked. "Then I'm glad I convinced him to eat the food."

"Thank you, Cade," she said with emotion clogging her throat. "You don't know what this means to me."

When his eyes met hers, he winked. "It's the least I could do after all you sacrificed to help Tilly last night."

Her heart grew warmer. "You really are an amazing man, Cade Hamilton."

"I think you should go lie down and rest a few hours."

She shook her head. "I can't. I have too much to do today."

His gaze narrowed on her. "Were you going to the bank?"

"The bank?" Her mind swam in confusion. Why would he think that?

"Your friend, yesterday. She said that she'd see you when you came to the bank."

Rebecca! How could Carrie have forgotten about her? "Oh, yes. The bank. I suppose I was going. Her mother works at the bank, and Rebecca told me her mother found something of Michael's that she thought I would like."

"Do you mind if I go with you? I need to stop at the mercantile and purchase some things."

Her heart skipped with excitement, bringing her more awake. This would be her first trip into town with her new husband. Although she couldn't wait to introduce him to her friends, she also didn't want to explain why he didn't want to be a doctor.

"Um, yes. Of course, you can come," she said, trying to keep the enthusiasm in her voice even if it was dwindling fast. She shouldn't feel let down that he didn't want to be a doctor. Instead, she should be elated that he was an attentive husband and that he wanted to help her with PJ. Indeed, Cade Hamilton was one in a million, and it shouldn't matter at all that he wasn't a doctor. He was *her* doctor, and he had helped Tilly and would help PJ if needs be, she was certain of it.

He motioned toward the bedroom. "Why don't you take a nap until Tilly wakes up? She can watch PJ while we go into town."

She nodded, feeling again the effect of very little sleep on her body. "I will. Thank you."

As much as she wanted to kiss him to show him her appreciation, she didn't know if now was the right time. Michael had once told her when were the right times to kiss a husband – and when were not the right times.

Her mind came to a halt, and she clenched her teeth. She wasn't married to Michael any longer, so why was she still allowing him to control her thoughts and actions? Well, she would change that… starting now!

Carrie quickly bent and kissed Cade on the lips. He hitched a breath, but the surprise didn't last long because he grasped her arm to pull her closer. Instead of a quick peck as she'd intended to give him, the gentle kiss continued, even though she was still standing, and he was in the chair with PJ on his lap.

Her hammering heart made her limbs weak, and for the life of her, she wanted to be the one sitting on his lap instead of her precious son. She lifted her hand to Cade's face and softly caressed his cheek before sliding her fingers through his hair – that was surprisingly not bristly like her first husband.

Although she had fought the impulse of comparing the two men before, she wouldn't any longer. Cade had so many good qualities, he was now outshining Michael in almost every way.

When PJ started fussing, Carrie hesitantly pulled away. Cade's eyes had turned a darker green – a gaze filled with desire. She hoped he could see that in her eyes, too.

"What was that for?" he asked.

She swallowed hard, trying to bring moisture to her suddenly dry throat. "Isn't that what wives do when they appreciate their husbands?"

One side of his mouth stretched higher than the other when he grinned. "I'm not sure, but Mrs. Hamilton, you can do that to me any time you'd like."

A flutter took over in her chest, making it hard to breathe. "Then you'd better count on it because I will."

As she walked to her bedroom, she wondered if she would get any sleep now. Her mind was wide awake, and she'd be dreaming of ways she could show her affection to her new husband.

NINE

Cade whistled a happy tune as Carrie sat beside him on her wagon's seat on their way toward the bank. The little nap she'd had this morning had done wonders to her state of mind. Of course, the kiss helped the most. Since that affectionate kiss, she'd been walking in heavenly bliss.

For this afternoon jaunt into town, Carrie picked out a ravishing dark blue jacket over her white blouse and black skirt. She had fixed her hair the same way as that first day when she married Cade only because she enjoyed the way his warm gaze slid over her when she wore her hair hanging over her shoulders and down her back.

Since she'd awakened from her nap, Cade had been looking at her differently. The butterflies dancing in her stomach made her wonder if he thought of making her his wife in the Biblical sense. She felt it was time to move forward instead of dwelling in the past.

Now, she couldn't wait for the sun to go down...

But first, she had to get this visit at the bank over with. Her nerves were jumpy, already sitting so close to Cade on the buckboard seat, bumping her arm against his with every movement of the vehicle. But now she wondered what Mrs. Sterling could possibly have found that was Michael's. When he worked at the bank, he never took anything personal from home, except for his lunch.

When Cade's whistling ended, she glanced at him. His twinkling gaze made her heart skip a beat, and his smile nearly melted her senseless.

"Tilly is finally getting more color back in her face," Carrie said, breaking the brief silence.

He nodded. "She told me that she's feeling better. I can see it in her eyes."

"I just wish her cough didn't sound so awful."

"That's to be expected."

As she stared at him, she wished he would be more open with his life, especially when it came to why he had decided not to practice medicine. Somehow, she needed to coax it out of him.

Carrie placed her arm on his thigh and gazed into his remarkable green eyes. Her heart jumped in her chest because of the personal way she was touching him, but by his expression, she could see that he enjoyed the closeness, too.

"Cade? Will you please tell me why you decided to quit being a doctor?"

His expression changed slightly, and hesitation was in his eyes. She held her breath, hoping her heartfelt plea would do the trick and start him talking.

He sighed heavily. "I suppose it's time to talk."

Relief flooded through her. "Yes, it is."

"A few months before I answered your newspaper advertisement, I was taking care of a little boy who was ill. Every kind of medicine I gave him only made him worse. Up until this point in my career, I had been curing people and fixing broken bones… and even delivering babies. But when I realized I couldn't do anything to save Clarence's life, I realized I wasn't the doctor everyone believed me to be. That's when I decided I couldn't let another person die under my care, so I left the practice and decided to take up farming."

Her heart wrenched. "Oh, but Cade," she turned toward him on the seat a little better, "don't you understand that it wasn't your fault at all? You did everything you could, which means the Lord wanted him back home. And you know as well as I that you can't argue with the Almighty. The Lord knows you were trying to save the boy's life, and if the Lord didn't think it was time to bring Clarence home, the boy would still be alive."

Sadness etched in Cade's eyes. "I understand what you're saying, my dear Carrie, but I..."

"Cade," she said, interrupting him. "Remember, you are only a doctor. You aren't God. You can't fix everyone's illness."

He released another sigh as he turned and looked back toward the road. She said a silent prayer that he would understand what she was trying to tell him. He couldn't expect to save everyone. That was God's responsibility.

After a few minutes of silence, Carrie faced forward in her seat. They approached a familiar building, and her stomach twisted in uncertainty. "There's the bank." She pointed to the red-bricked building on their left.

Cade pulled the horse to a stop and set the brake on the wagon. He hopped down and turned to lift her out. She bracketed her hands on his shoulders, and as he lifted her, their gazes locked. She couldn't read his expression very well, but he was still confused about his feelings as a doctor from what she could tell. Her heart ached to make him see, but just as God answered prayers, this particular issue would have to be worked out in Cade's time, not hers.

When her feet touched the ground, she stepped away from Cade. His smile looked forced. "The mercantile is right down that way. I won't be long at the bank, and I can meet you at the store when I'm finished."

"Are you certain?" He cupped the side of her face. "Because I don't mind."

She wanted to sigh with pleasure. Whether it was his soft touch or his sweet, caring words, she didn't know. One thing she did know, however, was that she liked this man more and more every day. Dare she say, *love*? Perhaps not yet, but it would happen shortly, she was certain.

"Don't be silly, Cade. I'll be fine."

He arched an eyebrow. "Something is worrying you, and that concerns me."

How could she not fall in love with this man? She tried to remember if Michael had ever been this attentive, and... she didn't think he had. "I haven't stepped foot inside the bank since Michael died, and well, I suppose I'm nervous about dredging up the past. I'd rather not think about those days."

"Then, I'll wait right here for you until you're done." Cade leaned against the wagon and folded his arms.

She chuckled. "Really, Cade. I can do this on my own. I'll meet you at the mercantile. Besides, I want to talk to Mrs. Sterling for a few minutes. I'm saddened by their moving out of Last Chance."

He nodded and straightened, dropping his hands by his sides. "Then, I'll let you do this by yourself." He leaned closer and kissed her forehead. "Don't be too long."

As he turned and hopped back in the wagon, her heartbeat quickened again, but this time it was for different reasons. She didn't want to go into the bank, but if it were something that must be done in order to get Michael out of her heart once and for all, then she'd do it.

Taking a deep breath, she courageously walked toward the bank with her head held high and her shoulders straight as though ready for battle. She knew there would certainly be a battle in her head and heart.

As she walked inside, her chest tightened as if something was suffocating her. *You can do this!* Had

Michael turned her into a weak woman? She didn't recall being this afraid to face her fears. Then again, she hadn't many fears growing up.

Only two patrons were in the bank talking with Mrs. Turnpike. Carrie glanced over at the other desk. Mrs. Sterling was sitting behind the desk, leaning over the table as she gathered papers. The older woman glanced up, and when she saw Carrie, a broad smile stretched across her wrinkled face.

"Oh, heavens. You came!" Mrs. Sterling jumped up from her chair and bustled toward Carrie, her arms stretched out in greeting. "Bless your heart for coming."

Carrie hugged the other lady, trying to keep a smile on her face. "Rebecca told me you were going to move soon, and I knew I had to come and see you."

Mrs. Sterling's eyes watered, and she dabbed a white hanky to the corner of her eyes. "I really don't want to leave, but... we cannot stay here now."

Carrie nodded. "I understand completely."

"Rebecca tells me you are remarried."

Cade's face popped into her mind, and she smiled. "Yes. Mr. Hamilton is a very nice man, and my son is already taken with him."

"How wonderful. Thank the Lord. I'm sure there have been miracles all around."

"Yes, I'm sure there have been." Carrie twisted her hands.

"Well, just the other day, I was going through some old cupboards here at the bank, trying to organize things before I leave, and I found something that had belonged to Michael." Mrs. Sterling moved to the far corner of the bank and dug through a box on the floor. She pulled out a journal and brought it back. "I remember my Wilbur telling me that Michael wrote quite often in his journal at work. Wilbur found it strange that Michael would do that here and not at home but," she shrugged, "who is to say if that's right or wrong."

"Exactly." With a trembling hand, she took the journal from the older woman. Michael had never told her that he had a journal, which told Carrie that whatever he wrote in that book was something he didn't want her knowing about. Ever.

"Thank you, Mrs. Sterling. I'll treasure this forever." But what Carrie didn't want to say aloud was that treasure was usually buried… although she thought this book might work better in the fireplace.

The older woman gave Carrie another hug before she left the bank. It wouldn't take her long to walk to the mercantile, but her curiosity about what was inside the journal got the better of her, and she moved around the building. She stopped under a tree, flipped open the book, and glanced at what was written on page fourteen.

"It is one day before my wedding to Carrie, but my heart is still with Parker Jo. I had promised my parents not to marry beneath my class, and yet, I find myself yearning to see Parker Jo more and more now. It's said that we want what we cannot have, and I am experiencing that now. Even though I will go through with marrying the woman my parents love, I will never be able to love Carrie as much as I love Parker Jo."

Reading Michael's words in his own handwriting finally brought her to reality. Before, she had just wondered about this other woman, especially since Cade had mentioned knowing a woman with that name. But now the truth was in front of Carrie, and it didn't make it any easier to handle. She must. If he hadn't loved her, why was she wasting her sorrow and broken heart on him?

She turned back a few more pages to see what he'd written earlier in the journal.

"I met the most amazing woman today. She volunteers at the hospital, and she has such a kind heart. I already know my parents won't approve of Parker Jo because she doesn't come from a wealthy family. I will try to convince them otherwise."

Carrie flipped forward another couple of pages.

"I'm living a double life. I'm courting a sweet woman, but I'm in love with another. I will probably marry Carrie, but Parker Jo is the one I want."

Carrie blinked back tears. Michael didn't deserve them.

"Something terrible happened today. I killed a man. Although it was purely accidental, and I ran him over with my carriage, there was no way I could help the poor man. Parker Jo was with me, and I didn't want anyone to know that I was secretly seeing her while engaged to Carrie. I will hold this guilt for a long time, and I pray for his family. I'd heard that Mr. Hamilton was an accountant."

Shock buzzed through her, and she dropped the book, slapping a hand over her mouth to keep from screaming. Michael had killed Cade's father?

Her legs weakened, and she sat on the ground in front of the tree, not caring that her dress would become wet from the snow, and she might get a chill. All she could think about was how to tell Cade. She couldn't possibly keep this secret from her new husband. She must tell him. Yet, she worried that he might blame her in some way. How could he stay married to her, knowing that her first husband killed Cade's father?

It just wasn't done! Cade would want the marriage annulled as soon as possible.

TEN

Something was wrong. Cade could feel it all around Carrie. She tried to act like she was fine and that her visit with Mrs. Sterling went smoothly, but Carrie's silence during the ride home told him things were not *fine*.

If she didn't want to talk to him, he couldn't force her, but how he wished she would tell him what happened inside the bank. A few times during the ride back to the house, he'd tried to get her to tell him what happened, but her answers were short, ending the conversation quickly. Her gaze wasn't on the road, nor was it on him. Instead, she studied the snow-covered landscape while frowning.

Cade's heart wrenched for her, knowing she was in agony somehow. If only she'd let him comfort her. After this morning's kiss, he had hoped that tonight would be the night when he could be a *real* husband. He assumed she wouldn't argue since she'd been looking differently at him. But now…

He'd probably be the one sleeping on the couch tonight.

The good mood he'd had all morning waned quickly. It had surprised him when PJ allowed Cade to feed him this morning, and he could see the little boy was warming up to him. So was the boy's mother. So perhaps, Cade needed to do something tonight to help Carrie relax so that she would warm up to him, too.

After watching her care for her maid, and PJ and seeing the care in Carrie's eyes when she was visiting with her friend, Cade knew Carrie would make a very good wife.

And since he'd had a sample of her kiss, he was quite eager to claim his husbandly rights. He'd already realized that once he had her in his arms, she melted. He'd make it a point to get her that way this evening.

He stopped the wagon in front of the house and hopped down. As he reached up to help her, she turned and climbed out of the wagon on the other side. Cade frowned. No, she was not fine at all.

Hurrying around the wagon to catch up to her, he noticed she quickened her step. Cade grasped her arm before she could enter the house. As he swung her around to face him, tears were brimming in her eyes.

"Oh, my darling, Carrie. Please tell me what's wrong."

"I… can't." Her throat jumped in what looked to be a hard swallow. "You wouldn't understand."

"Are you upset because of Michael?"

She nodded and pursed her lips.

"How do you know I won't understand?" He loosened his grip on her arms as he slowly pulled her closer. "Give me a chance to be an understanding husband."

Carrie blinked rapidly. "Why, Cade? You came to Last Chance knowing that there was a possibility that you were marrying in name only."

He tried not to get upset. After all, something was eating her up inside. He needed to find out what it was. "I could say the same thing about you, my darling, but the kisses we have shared so far have told me otherwise." He arched an eyebrow. "Am I wrong? Did I misread you when you kissed me?"

"I shouldn't have," she said in a rush. "I was caught up in the moment, and now I realize I shouldn't have kissed you."

"No, Carrie." Cade pulled her closer, and she pressed her hands against his chest as though wanting to stop him.

He couldn't let her. They needed to be closer so that she would melt in his arms and let him comfort her. "You cannot tell me it wasn't real. There is something between us, and kissing you has only confirmed what I'd been feeling."

She stopped struggling as her gaze locked with his. "What… have you been feeling?"

Heavens, this wasn't the time – or the place – to tell her his feelings. He wanted her to open up to him first. Then again, maybe he needed to take the plunge this time. Perhaps then, she would tell him what was bothering her.

He cupped the side of her face as his thumb gently stroked her cheek. "Carrie, as I've gotten to know you these past few days, I've realized you are the kind of woman I want as my wife, and I want you to be the mother of our children."

Cade watched her closely, hoping to see her expression of delight. Instead, she became angry and pushed his hand away. "That's never going to happen, Mr. Hamilton."

She moved away from him so quickly that he didn't have time to grab her again. Of course, her statement surprised him and wrenched his heart. What was she talking about? He knew she felt the sparks of attraction between them. He just needed to bring it back.

Yet, everything went topsy-turvy when she entered the bank. Cade wasn't going to give up. He could make this right. No, he *would* make this right.

* * * *

Carrie rushed into the house. Unshed tears burned her eyes, but she had promised herself she wouldn't cry. Right now, she was more angry and sad. She didn't know how she could take her anger out on Michael, but he was the one who deserved her wrath. Poor Cade had just been caught in the crossfire.

Right away, she heard PJ's crying. It was different this time. Panicked, she hurried into his bedroom. Tilly sat on the rocking chair, trying to soothe the baby, but the worried look in her eyes let Carrie know something was wrong. She quickly took PJ away from the maid, holding her boy close to her bosom. He was warm. Much too warm.

Pressing her cheek against the boy's forehead, Carrie realized he had a fever. She pulled back and studied his pale face with blotches of red patches. Her stomach twisted. She prayed he hadn't gotten sick like Tilly.

She smiled at PJ the best she could, not wanting to worry him. "Mommy is here." She lovingly stroked his warm cheek.

"Oh, Carrie," Tilly said in a tight voice. "I tried cooling him down, but I didn't dare do anything without Mr. Hamilton around to let me know if it was right."

"What's right?" Cade stepped into the house, closing the door behind him. As soon as his attention landed on Carrie and PJ, he rushed to them. Cade placed his hand on the boy's head. Cade's worried gaze met hers.

"Do you think he has pneumonia?" she asked shakily.

"He wouldn't get it unless having a chest cold first. But, it's obvious he has some kind of infection inside his body that needs to come out."

Fear nearly choked the air right out of Carrie's lungs. But she must be strong for her son. "Cade… can you help him?"

His defeated expression let her know that he didn't have faith in himself. That scared her to death.

"Cade, please," she begged. "I know you can do this."

Confusion flickered across his expression, but then he inhaled deeply and nodded. "Go into the kitchen and sit. I will need to get some instruments from my medical bag so that I can examine him."

Carrie sighed with relief. "Thank you, Cade."

She hurried into the kitchen and sat on a chair. PJ continued to cry, which made her heart break. She hated feeling so helpless. Cooing to him, she stroked his face, but that didn't seem to calm him in the least. A few red rashes were on his cheeks and forehead.

Closing her eyes, she said a silent prayer, asking God to guide Cade to find PJ's ailment. Although Cade didn't think he could do it, she knew he could. He'd been a respected doctor at one time. He just needed a little nudge to move in the right direction.

She glanced at her baby. Would PJ be Cade's *nudge*? She just hoped her son would get well soon.

Cade walked into the kitchen and placed his medical bag on the table. He first used his stethoscope to listen to PJ's breathing. Carrie studied Cade's worried face, hoping to see signs that nothing was terribly wrong with her son.

Once Cade was finished listening to PJ's breathing, he then looked inside her son's mouth. PJ fussed and wiggled, but she tried her best to hold him still. It took a few minutes longer, but then finally, Cade finished. He ran his fingers over PJ's face and down his neck. Finally, he sighed and shook his head, meeting Carrie's gaze.

"I don't know what it is. PJ is breathing just fine. In fact, he's got some healthy lungs. His throat doesn't appear to be red, and his throat isn't swollen." Cade shrugged. "I don't know why he has a fever."

Carrie's worry escalated. This wasn't what she had wanted to hear. There must be a reason. "What else could cause him to act like this?"

Cade shook his head, frowning. "I don't know. We will just have to wait a few days to see if more symptoms show up. Seeing the symptoms will help me to know how to help PJ."

"What should I do about his fever?"

"I won't be able to pack him in the snow as I did with Tilly, so for now, just get wet cloths and put them on his head and under his arms." Cade touched PJ's head again. "I'll monitor him closely for the next few days."

Carrie didn't like the sound of that, but what else could she do? There was no doubt about it. She would stay by PJ's side night and day until they found out why he was sick.

ELEVEN

Cade trudged on tired legs out to the barn to milk the goat and collect the eggs. The mornings were growing colder, and Thanksgiving was nearly upon them. While he was at the mercantile, he asked if they were going to order turkeys. The owner had mentioned that Pastor Collins would be bringing some into town in the next day or so. Cade wanted to do something special for Carrie, and Thanksgiving would be the perfect opportunity.

He still couldn't figure out her attitude change. Something had happened at the bank, yet, she wasn't willing to talk about it. Two days had passed since that day, and she'd spent most of her time in PJ's room. Cade kept waiting for the little boy to cough or to show any signs of what his malady was, but nothing. Thankfully, the boy's fever wasn't very high, but PJ hadn't wanted to eat much, and when he did, he gagged. The boy was very ornery, no matter who was holding him.

Thankfully, Tilly was feeling better, and so she helped Cade make the meals. From the chats he had with Carrie's maid, he wondered if Tilly was used to making the meals, anyway. He wanted to laugh. Cade should have realized Carrie wouldn't know how. Her parents had never taught her to do *real* work.

He carried the milk and the eggs into the kitchen, where Tilly was busy preparing the morning meal.

"Carrie is awake if you wanted to go check on her and PJ," the older woman said.

"I need to collect some firewood first."

Tilly nodded and turned back to her bowl of oatmeal. As Cade left the house again, he bundled his collar around his neck. It certainly was nippier here in Nebraska than it was in New York. It must have something to do with the elevation.

He moved back to the barn where he'd kept the supply of freshly-cut firewood, and just before reaching the door, he noticed a woman walking toward the house. She was bundled in a fur-lined coat and had heavy boots on her feet. A fur-lined cap covered most of her blonde hair.

When she noticed him looking at her, she smiled and waved. "Doctor Hamilton?"

Inwardly, he groaned. Carrie had told everyone he was a doctor? But of course, she had. He hadn't told her otherwise until after he had arrived in town. He didn't know how he could break the bad news to this woman coming to see him.

"I'm Cade Hamilton." He smiled and met her halfway.

"I'm Heather Barnes." She put forth her gloved right hand, and he shook it. "I'm a midwife here in Last Chance. It's nice to meet you."

"Are you a friend of Carrie's?" he asked.

"Oh, yes. Our numbers are few here in Last Chance, and so we make sure we're all friends. Since the blizzard, we've all learned to rely on each other for support."

"That's a very good thing to do. All of you have been brave during these hard times."

"Yes, they have been trying for all of us." She motioned toward the house. "Is Carrie at home?"

"Yes. Her baby has been sick the past few days, and she's been with him nonstop."

Mrs. Barnes' eyes widened. "Oh, dear. What is wrong?"

Cade didn't know how to answer. If he said *I don't know,* he made himself look like a fool because he'd gone to school to be a doctor, yet he didn't know what was wrong with PJ. "I think it might be his ears." Cade supposed that was a good enough answer because really, it could be his ears, although there had been no discharge from them.

"Oh, the poor little dear. Do you mind if I go inside?"

Once again, he didn't know how to answer. He hated looking like a complete idiot. "Sure, let me take you inside."

He'd gather the wood later.

The woman didn't say anything as he walked inside the house and to PJ's room. Cade gently knocked on the door and then opened it slightly and peeked inside. Carrie was rocking her son, and he seemed to be playing with a toy on her lap. At least the child wasn't crying as he'd been doing so much of lately.

When Carrie turned her head to look at him, he motioned over his shoulders. "You have a visitor."

Carrie's hair had been combed and pulled back into a ponytail. She wore one of her simpler blue dresses today. "Who?" she asked.

"Mrs. Barnes." He opened the door wider to let the other woman inside.

Carrie's face brightened, and she quickly stood, keeping PJ in her arms. "Oh, Heather. It's so wonderful to see you."

The two women gave one-arm hugs. Immediately, Mrs. Barnes touched PJ's face. She frowned.

"He's warm." Mrs. Barnes glanced at Cade.

"Yes, he's had a small fever off and on for the past two days. He's had a rash, and he's sick to his stomach off and on throughout the day."

Mrs. Barnes nodded. "It could be an ear infection."

Carrie gasped and looked toward Cade. "Could it be?"

"Perhaps, but he's had no discharge come out of his ears."

Carrie's shoulders drooped. "Rats." She sighed and looked back at her friend. "I just don't know what is wrong with my son."

"Do you mind if I look him over?" Mrs. Barnes asked.

Immediately, warning bells shot off in Cade's mind. The woman was a *midwife*, for heaven's sake. What is she going to know that a doctor won't? Although he wanted to stop her, Carrie seemed to welcome the idea. Once again, doubts filled his mind. She didn't believe in him, even though she said she would.

Disappointed and feeling highly rejected, he turned and left the two women, heading back into the kitchen. Tilly's questioning gaze met his.

"What does Mrs. Barnes want?" the older woman asked.

"Just to visit," he grumbled, "although, she wants to examine PJ, too." Cade sat at the table, resting his elbows on the hardwood.

"Mr. Hamilton?" Tilly stepped closer, stopping at the end of the table. "I'm here if you need someone to listen to your woes."

He gave her a pitiful grin. "My woes?"

"Yes, sir. It's obvious that something is bothering you." She patted his shoulder. "Give her time. She'll come around."

"*Come around?*"

"Yes. Carrie likes you, I can tell, but she's still grieving Michael. But soon, she'll see that you are much better than Michael."

He wrinkled his forehead and narrowed his gaze on the older woman. "Am I correct in assuming you didn't like the man?"

Tilly shrugged and moved to the stove. "Let's just say that I thought Carrie could have done better."

Curious to what the maid really meant, he moved away from the table and stood next to her at the stove. "Go on."

"Well, it was Michael's idea to move out here. He knew Carrie was a city girl, but he sweet-talked her into coming out here to prairie land. Carrie had no idea how to be a prairie wife. But over the next few years, as I watched them together, I noticed that he criticized her more than I thought he should have. Michael pointed out her flaws, which he had already known about. I think he wanted her to be like the other wives in town, but Carrie wasn't." Tilly turned her head to look at him. "And something was missing in his eyes when he looked at Carrie."

"Missing? Like what?"

"Love."

Surprise washed over him. "He didn't love her?"

Tilly shrugged and continued to stir the oatmeal cooking in the pot on the hot stove. "I rarely heard him say it to her. She told him that she loved him all the time, but he would smile and kiss her forehead and either leave the room or change the subject."

Cade's heart wrenched. How could Michael have acted like that? Then again, Carrie had figured something out about why Michael named their son, Parker Joe – after a woman. That was when Carrie had started acting differently about her dead husband. Had she realized Michael hadn't loved her after all? Cade wondered what the man's excuse was for being married five years, and yet they only had a one-year-old child.

The more Cade learned about Michael Porter, the more he wished the man was alive so that he could punch him in the face. Carrie was a sweet woman with a kind heart. So, she didn't know how to plant a garden or... cook a meal. There were other good qualities about her, and it took a man like Cade to see them.

"Thank you for telling me, Tilly. I promise not to treat her that way."

Tilly gave him a wide grin. "Oh, I know you won't, Mr. Hamilton. I've seen the way you've been looking at her lately, and Michael has *never* looked at her that way."

Although excitement shot through him to think he might have a chance to convince her that they were meant to be together, his heart still ached that she had been in such a pathetic marriage.

He stepped away, but then Tilly grasped his arm, stopping him. "One more thing," she said.

"What's that?"

"Don't you let that Mrs. Barnes in there try to tell you she knows more about doctorin' than you do." Tilly nodded sharply. "All she knows is how to deliver babies."

Cade chuckled softly. Maybe Tilly had read his mind earlier, after all. "If you say so."

"Oh, I do say so." She straightened her shoulder and lifted her chin. "There was no way that woman would have known how to treat my pneumonia. I would have died if not for you."

He loved hearing those words, even though he doubted they were true. Tilly could have probably overcome her sickness in time. Then again, she'd had a very high fever, so maybe…

His mind halted as realization struck. Had he been a good doctor after all? If only he could believe that.

He pushed the thought aside. He'd think about that later. Right now, however, he needed to find answers about Carrie's sudden attitude shift. So… while she was in the nursery visiting with her friend, maybe Cade should do some snooping through her drawers to see if he could find anything that would help him understand his wife.

TWELVE

Cade was still awake when Carrie left PJ's room. Her son had finally allowed her to place him in his bed and walk out the door without crying. Her arms ached from holding him so much, but her heart hurt more. Not knowing what was causing his ailment bothered her more than she could understand. She was the mother. She should know what was wrong with her own child.

As she took quiet steps toward Cade, sitting on the couch in the living room as he stared at the full fire in the hearth, her heart hurt again, but differently this time. She had wanted to love him, but she feared his rejection. She hadn't planned on telling him about Michael's confession, yet, if Cade ever found out, he'd hate her. She wouldn't be able to handle that, especially if PJ looked up to him as a father.

The best way for keeping her heart – and the heart of her son – intact was not to love Cade at all. Yet, could they stay married and live in the same house without that deep bond?

What needed to happen was to tell Cade the truth. Then, he could have the marriage annulled and leave town. Or she could take PJ and return to New York to live with her parents.

That, right there, might be the best course of action.

She moved past Cade to sit on the couch. He continued to stare at the fire. The frown on his face was deep. She couldn't tell if he was angry or sad. She waited a few moments for him to say something, but he didn't. It was up to her to start this most awkward and disheartening conversation.

Rubbing her nervous hands together, she collected her thoughts, trying to breathe calmly. "PJ finally let me lay him down in his bed."

Cade's expression remained the same as he stared at the fire. "Hopefully, he can sleep better tonight."

"That's my hope, too."

"And how are you holding up?"

"I'm exhausted physically and emotionally."

He nodded, not moving his stare. "As would any good Mother be."

His nonchalant attitude worried Carrie. Cade wasn't usually like this. Her stomach twisted, wishing she didn't care about him so much. "Yes, I suppose any good Mother would feel like that."

Her hands turned colder due to her nerves, so she left the couch and stood in front of the hearth, letting the heat from the fire warm her. She glanced over her shoulder at Cade. He still had a blank stare as he watched the flames licking up the brick wall.

"Cade? Is something amiss?"

He didn't budge, and he didn't answer for a few seconds. "Why would anything be amiss?"

She wanted to scream and shake some sense into him. "Cade, look at me." Finally, his gaze lifted to her face, but his expression stayed the same. "What is wrong?" she asked.

"What makes you think something is wrong?"

"Cade Hamilton," she snapped, turning and folding her arms across her bosom. "Your answers are driving me mad. Will you just tell me what's wrong."

He arched an eyebrow. At least he wasn't giving her the same look. "Tell *you* what's wrong? So, you're telling me that I should open up to you, but you aren't going to open up to me?"

Perhaps she had deserved his bitter tone. After all, she had been withdrawn, especially since reading Michael's journal. "What do you want me to tell you?"

He exhaled slowly. "Let's start by telling me why all of a sudden, you want to change your son's name and why your grieving came to a quick stop."

Cade was correct. She needed to tell him *everything*. "When you had mentioned your friend, Parker Jo, and where you met her, I started putting the puzzle pieces together in my mind about when Michael had wanted to name our baby. A few things had happened during my pregnancy that, at the time, didn't seem odd, but they did after our conversation. I had realized that Michael had been in love with Parker Jo. It wasn't until recently when I discovered that he had wanted to marry her, but his parents didn't approve of the match. That is why he married me... because I came from the right kind of background."

Cade nodded and scratched his chin. "All right. That makes sense as to why you would want to change your son's name."

Her breath was still ragged as she tried to build up the courage to tell him more. "That day is when I decided Michael didn't deserve my grieving." She paced the floor, from one wall to the other, in front of Cade. "I knew I should move forward with my new life." She stopped in front of him. "That's why I'd acted the way I did."

"That's why you let me kiss you?"

"Yes."

"And then the next time, you kissed me."

She nodded.

"And yet, the day we went into town when you returned from the bank, you were completely different."

A knot of emotion caught in her throat. "Yes."

"I want you to tell me why."

I can't tell him... Inwardly, Carrie's mind fought a battle with her heart. She *must* tell him the truth no matter how it would hurt her – and him.

She licked her dry lips. "Mrs. Sterling found a journal Michael had kept at the bank."

Cade didn't remove his stare from her, which made her heart pound harder.

"I left the bank and opened it. I'd realized Michael was indeed in love with Parker Jo and that that hadn't changed after he married me. I also stumbled across another entry." She swallowed, although it was difficult. "He'd been driving a carriage and hit an older man. In his journal, Michael wrote that he didn't stop because Parker Jo was with him, and he didn't want anyone to see them together. He later found out who the man was that he'd hit." She inhaled shakily. "He knew the man was an accountant... Mr. Hamilton."

Cade's lips tightened in a straight line, and his eyes misted. He bunched his hands into fists. His chest rose and fell quickly. Carrie waited for him to say something because she wasn't sure if he wanted her to go on. However, she wasn't finished with her confession.

She licked her dry lips again. "Upon reading that journal entry, I crumbled to the ground and cried. I was so afraid to tell you."

"Why?"

"Because... I had feelings for you, and even PJ was starting to take to you. I knew that if I told you that my deceased husband killed your father, that you wouldn't be able to live with me any longer." She brushed away a stray tear rolling down her cheek. "I'm prepared to let you seek an annulment."

"Is that what you want?"

She shook her head. "I don't want to stay married to a man who can't stand to look at me because of what Michael did."

Slowly, Cade stood and stepped in front of her. "Were you married to Michael at the time of the accident?"

"No, but we were engaged."

"Then you had no control over what Michael did or didn't do. Correct?"

"Well, I suppose."

He shrugged. "You said he was with Parker Jo at the time, so I can assume you didn't have control over that."

"Of course, not." Her voice broke. "I had no clue he was still seeing his former love."

"Then why should I blame you, Carrie?" Cade's expression relaxed, and he cupped the side of her face. "I would never blame you for something you didn't even know about."

She wanted to cry with relief, but she'd done enough crying these past few months that would last her a lifetime. "Do you forgive me?"

"For what Michael did?" He shook his head. "There's nothing to forgive on that matter. However, I do forgive you for not telling me right away."

She hiccuped a laugh. "Yes, I'm sorry about that. I was so conflicted. My heart was breaking because I thought our marriage was over."

Slowly, a smile stretched across his face. "Your heart was breaking over that?" He winked. "Now that is a good thing. That tells me that you like me as much as I like you, and it tells me that you want to work on our marriage just as much as I do."

"Yes, I do, Cade." She stepped closer to him, gingerly, laying her hands on his chest. "In just a little time, I've realized how much better you have treated me than the man I'd been married to for five years."

He was quiet for a few moments, staring at her with his dreamy green eyes.

"Carrie? I need to know… do you feel that way about me because I'm a doctor?"

She shook her head. "What you learned in school doesn't make you the man you are today. What defines you is your giving heart and willingness to help a woman and her child who were down on their luck and needed help." She smiled wider. "You've come a long way since we were children."

"And to think, I was the one who used to pull your pigtails."

She chuckled. "And now, you are the one who is pulling on my heartstrings."

"That's all right," he whispered as he wrapped his arms around her. "Because you are pulling on mine, too."

"You know," she said huskily, "I'd never realized what I'd been missing in my first marriage until I met you."

"And what was that?" His voice lowered as he stared at her mouth.

"Affection."

"Oh, my darling, Carrie, I promise to make up for what you've lost."

When their lips met, the kiss turned passionate almost immediately. Carrie clung to him as she responded to his urgent kiss, hoping to show him exactly what her heart was doing at this very moment.

Once again, she compared Cade to her first husband, and once again, Cade had left Michael in the dust. Why had she never noticed that when Michael kissed her, it wasn't passionate? Why hadn't Carrie noticed that when Michael held her, it wasn't so close she could feel the beat of his heart against her bosom? But now that she realized this, she never wanted to let Cade go. He completed her, and she'd never felt more like a desirable woman than she did right now.

Heavens, he was such a good kisser, and she was proud to know that he was hers – forever.

"Carrie," he muttered as his lips trailed from her mouth down her neck. "May I suggest we move this into our bedroom?"

Tingles multiplied over her body as her heart sang with happiness. "If you don't, I will."

He chuckled and lifted her into his arms. Gasping from surprise, she wrapped her arms around his neck.

"Cade? What are you doing?"

"Well, the first time I carried you over the threshold after we were married, you had passed out on the lawn." He grinned. "I thought I'd do it the correct way this time."

"Oh, Cade." Her heart melted. "You are the most amazing man."

"And you, my darling wife, are the most amazing woman I've ever met."

As he carried her toward their bedroom, she knew the moment was right. She anticipated becoming his wife in the most meaningful way. She had a feeling that Cade would surpass her first husband in this regard, as well.

They reached the bedroom, and he kicked the door closed with his foot. Carrie loved the look in his dreamy eyes, and for the first time, she felt truly loved. Michael had *never* looked at her that way.

But now it was time to forget about the man she had first married. From this point forward, the only man in her life would be Cade – until PJ reached that age, and then she'd have two men in her life.

Of course, having more children with Cade was something to consider. There was no better way to bring their family together.

Just as Cade placed her on the bed, PJ started crying from the nursery. Groaning, she closed her eyes and rubbed her forehead. It wouldn't be right to have Tilly mind the baby so that Carrie could get intimate with Cade. Apparently, they weren't supposed to consummate their marriage just yet.

Cade sighed, and his shoulders drooped. "I suppose this will have to wait until later."

Carrie nodded. "Yes, it will." She moved to stand, but he placed his hand on her shoulder, stopping her.

"You need your rest. Let me take care of PJ tonight."

Could she love her husband any more than she did at this moment? "Thank you. But if you get tired, come wake me up, and we'll switch."

He bent and kissed her briefly on the lips. "Sweet dreams, my darling."

As he walked out of the room, Carrie wondered how she'd gotten so lucky. Now, to make everything perfect, they just needed to figure out what was wrong with her son. She prayed Cade would remember his medical knowledge and find a cure for whatever was ailing poor PJ.

THIRTEEN

Cade hummed a song to little PJ in his arms while sitting in the rocking chair, moving slowly back and forth. The nursery lamp was low, as was the fire in the hearth, but Cade could still study the sick little boy's face. PJ had retained the same symptoms since that first day – low fever, clammy skin, red rashes all over his body, and a sick stomach. Of course, the queasy stomach and fever were never consistent.

There was also another symptom Cade noticed today. The boy was scratching his face and arms as though something bothered his skin. All of this was too confusing for Cade.

Earlier today, Tilly had mentioned that Mrs. Barnes would research these symptoms to see if she could discover what was wrong with PJ. Cade's gut twisted in annoyance. He really didn't want a *midwife* to be the doctor in this situation. *He* had taken the proper schooling to be a doctor, not her! And if he really thought about it, he wanted to do this – not only for PJ's sake but also because Cade didn't want Carrie to believe that he was a failure. It was bad enough that he thought that way about himself already.

Sighing, he closed his eyes. It wasn't easy to think straight when he and his new wife were about ready to become intimate. The passion in her eyes – and especially in her kiss – let him know how she felt. He wanted to erase every memory she had of Michael and replace them with blissful moments with her new husband.

It had thrilled him to know that she didn't just love him because of his medical background. Being a doctor had given him an oversize ego at one time, and he had believed that women desired him because of that. At first, Cade thought Carrie was like this, but he was happy to see she wasn't.

Because of that, he now wanted to make her proud. He didn't want Mrs. Barnes to take the credit if she found PJ's ailment. If Cade was going to be Last Chance's doctor, he didn't want them to doubt him even once. He *must* be the one who found a cure for whatever was wrong with PJ.

"Oh, Lord," Cade whispered, hoping to get help from the highest, "please help me. Guide my thoughts to that which I have learned so that I will know how to treat PJ."

He continued to rock the little boy in his arms as his mind returned to yesteryear. While living in Peru, Cade had studied for a few years, doing nothing but reading out of books and learning from pictures. Finally, he was allowed to follow a doctor in the local hospital to see what was done.

During this time, Cade asked as many questions as he could. Patients came in for all manner of ailments – from broken bones to Cholera, influenza, and even consumption. One time, they thought the town had been exposed to yellow fever, but thankfully, that wasn't the case.

Cade had gone from watching a doctor in a hospital to finally working beside Doctor Dawson. Brian Dawson was the best, in Cade's opinion. He was very friendly with his patients, and he teased and made the children laugh. Everyone loved that doctor, and Cade wanted to be just like him. He had been on his way to being a revered physician, but then when Clarence died, something inside Cade had been killed along with the boy.

However, Carrie's words filled his head. He had tried to be God. He shouldn't have taken on that responsibility. All Cade could be was God's *instrument*. And, right now, that was exactly what Cade wanted. God's help was the only way PJ would be cured.

PJ had stopped fussing and itching a half an hour ago, and finally, the boy was falling asleep again. Cade was tempted to lay the boy in his bed, but then he realized Carrie would more than likely be asleep when he came to bed. She needed rest, and he'd give it to her.

He groaned softly. Life was simpler when he was young and being raised on a farm. All he had to learn was how to take care of the animals, plant, and harvest. Cade had been good with the animals. He'd trained the horses, and cows had come to trust him.

As a boy, Cade had a dog – Rusty. The dog helped him herd sheep from time to time. Rusty had been Cade's best friend for the longest time. He had come to know that dog well, especially when he'd nearly killed him when Rusty was a pup.

Not knowing what dogs could eat – and especially, what they could *not* eat – Cade had given Rusty a taste of his eggs, and within hours, the dog became violently ill. Cade had learned quickly not to feed the dog from the table.

Cade's thoughts screeched to a halt. *Eggs!* He had fed PJ eggs the day he'd gotten sick. In fact, every day since Cade had fed that to the boy. What if the boy was allergic to that food? Carrie had mentioned that day she'd caught Cade feeding PJ that he had never eaten eggs before.

Excitement shot through Cade, and he sat up straighter. His mind continued to spin with memories of when he was a doctor working with Brian Dawson. A woman had come in to see Doctor Dawson, and her face was covered in a rash. Her face was pasty, and she had a small fever. She also complained of not keeping any food in her stomach since the night before. Doctor Dawson had diagnosed her as being allergic to shellfish.

Cade now knew how to treat PJ!

Slowly, he lifted out the chair and carried PJ out of the room. He tiptoed to Tilly's room, and thankfully, her light was on, which he could see from under the door. He knocked. "Tilly?"

Seconds later, he heard the floor creak as she walked toward the door. She opened the door but stood behind it, trying to hide her white nightgown. Her eyes were wide as she glanced from him to PJ.

"Do you need my help with the baby?"

"Yes. I think I know what's wrong with him, but we need to find stinging nettle. I know it's late, and there is snow on the ground, but—"

"I have some tea."

Cade stopped, not certain he heard correctly. "You have tea?"

"Yes. I have seasonal allergies, and so I have already prepared stinging nettle tea for whenever I need it."

Relief swept over him. *Thank you, Lord!* "We need it now. Get some ready, and we'll have PJ drink it."

She hurried back into her room and grabbed her wrapper. Within seconds, she was bustling out of the room and hurrying toward the kitchen. Cade turned up the kitchen lamp as Tilly found a kettle and placed it on the wood-burning stove, which, thankfully, was still warm from supper. Next, she opened a cupboard and withdrew a glass jar with the plant's cooked dried leaves.

"What do you think he's allergic to?" Tilly asked as she prepared the tea.

"Eggs."

She gasped. "I gave him some this morning."

"We have all given him some for the past few days."

"Why do you think that's it?"

Cade glanced down at PJ, who thankfully, was still asleep. Slowly, Cade moved to the kitchen table and sat on the chair. "When I was a young boy, I had given my dog an egg, and it made him really sick." He shrugged. "I just followed the strong instincts inside me that this was what happened to PJ."

"Oh, I pray you're right."

"You know…. I think I am." He smiled, feeling good about the decision. Of course, it was the Lord who put the idea in his head.

It took another fifteen minutes, but soon the water was warm enough to prepare the tea. Cade gently shook the baby awake, softly calling the boy's name. When PJ opened his eyes, he frowned and started scratching his arms in discomfort.

"Here, PJ," Cade said, bringing the teacup to the boy's mouth. "Drink this. It will make you feel better."

At first, PJ pushed it away, but when Tilly came over to assist, the boy followed directions. Gradually, he began to drink more until the cup was empty. Cade smiled at the boy and stroked a hand over the child's moist forehead. Cade knew it wouldn't work immediately, but soon, the boy would feel much better.

"Here," Tilly said, taking PJ out of Cade's arms, "let me watch him until he falls asleep. You look plum tired, Mr. Hamilton."

He felt exhausted, but it was more from knowing that he had figured out how to treat poor PJ.

"If you don't mind," he said with a smile, "I'd like to stay up just a little while longer and keep a watchful eye over my patient."

Tilly's eyes widened. "*Patient?*" She smiled. "Does that mean what I think it means?"

Chuckling, he moved beside the older woman and wrapped an arm around her shoulders. He leaned in and kissed PJ's forehead and then met Tilly's questioning stare.

"Yes. That means what you think it means."

"Oh, that's the best news ever, Mr... um, *Doctor* Hamilton."

His heartbeat flipped with happiness. It did feel good to be recognized as a doctor again.

"But I must say," Tilly continued, "how surprised I am that you'd use an herb to treat your patient instead of trying to force some of that nasty medicine down the boy's throat like normal doctors do."

"Actually, Tilly," he stepped away from the maid, "there's a good explanation for that. When I was working with another doctor, he showed me how to use the herbs method. We had several patients who wouldn't take the medications we gave them."

"That's just brilliant," Tilly cheered. "There was a reason you were guided toward Last Chance. This town needs great doctors like yourself."

Had the woman been correct? Was it Cade's fate to come to this town, especially with his knowledge of both types of medications? He wanted to think so. "Thank you, Tilly. It does my heart good to hear you say that." He kissed her cheek, and her face bloomed with color.

Tilly took PJ back into the nursery, and Cade went to the cupboard to find some regular tea for him. He needed something to keep him awake for another hour until he knew PJ was sleeping more comfortably. He found himself grinning the longer he thought of what Tilly said. Surprisingly, he was excited to start his practice in town. Of course, he didn't want to be away from his wife and son for very long, so perhaps he could build a little cabin out back on the land to be nearby. After all, he planned to have a large family with his wonderful wife.

He prepared his tea and walked back to the table and sat. He stared at his teacup while his mind spun with ideas. Getting started on his practice would have to begin soon. This town had been without a doctor for far too long.

A gentle hand touched his shoulder, mere seconds before he smelled Carrie's fragrance. He snapped out of his thoughts and looked at her standing next to him. Sleep was evident in her eyes, and he was happy that she had gotten a little rest.

"What are you doing out of bed?" he asked.

"I woke up suddenly. I don't know why, but when I peeked into the nursery, Tilly gave me the good news."

He nodded. "Yes, I figured out what was wrong with PJ." He turned and slid an arm around her waist, pulling her to sit on his lap. She came willingly and hooked her arms around his shoulders.

"I knew you could do it." She kissed his lips briefly.

"Thank you for having faith in me, even when I didn't have it."

Her smile softened, and she caressed his cheek. "Do you have it now?"

"I do." He tightened his arms around her. "And I've decided that I want to be the town's doctor."

Her pretty brown eyes twinkled. "Why?"

"Because it felt good to help cure someone. However, this time, I'll let God help me."

"That's the best way to do it."

Cade couldn't believe how beautiful she was, even with sleepy eyes and messy hair, he'd never seen anyone lovelier before – and he never would.

"Are you ready to come to bed?" she asked.

"Not yet. I'm going to monitor my patient first."

Sighing, she cuddled against him. He stroked his hand down her hair and back, loving the closeness. "I don't think I've told you, but," he kissed her forehead, "I'm very much in love with you, Mrs. Hamilton."

She tilted her head and looked into his eyes. "Good because I love you more and more each day."

When he kissed her, he knew this was the perfect way to stay awake while *monitoring* PJ. Of course, Cade would have to make sure nothing more happened until he and Carrie reached the bedroom. At least that would be in his immediate future.

EPILOGUE

"Happy Thanksgiving," Carrie said as she carried the cooked turkey to the table where her small family was gathered around. Both Tilly and PJ felt so much better, which made this very special day even more special. And... because Carrie cooked the turkey all by herself, this was definitely the year for accomplishments.

Thankfully, Tilly stood behind Carrie and watched her to make sure she did everything right. Starving her family wasn't a good thing to do.

Cade's evergreen eyes glistened with love when he looked at Carrie. He stood and kissed her briefly before taking the fork and carving knife in his hands. She sat, waiting for him to begin. Instead, he glanced around the table, looking at everyone for a few seconds before moving to the next person. Carrie had never seen him so happy.

"I want to thank you for accepting me into your home and into your lives." He rested his gaze on Carrie. "And thank you for loving me, unconditionally."

She touched his arm, smiling. "It's *you* who we should be thanking. You have come into our lives and literally saved each one of us."

"God is good," Tilly said with a nod. "We have been blessed."

"Indeed, He is." Cade placed the knife and fork down. "I think we should offer a prayer of thanks before we begin."

Carrie nodded, her heart growing larger than before. How had she gotten so lucky to marry this man?

"Doctor Hamilton?" Tilly asked. "Please, let me say the prayer."

"Of course."

Everyone closed their eyes, and as Tilly began to pray, Carrie peeked at her family. Although she'd not been loved in her first marriage, she had to experience all of that for a reason. During those five years, the trial God put her through was to help her grow stronger and accept *true* love when Cade came into her life. She also had to learn how to forgive and forget, and she was working on that with Michael right now. But she was so very grateful this year for her love that grew daily for Cade Hamilton.

Tilly ended the prayer, and everyone said *Amen*. As Cade started carving the turkey, the heavenly scent of a well-cooked bird wafted through the kitchen, making her stomach grumble. Tilly had helped her prepare other items for their meal, but Carrie was proud of herself for the turkey.

Cade took a piece of meat and plopped it into his mouth. Closing his eyes, he released a low groan of pleasure. "This is the best thing I've ever tasted."

This was another reason Carrie loved him so much. He was always so quick to praise her for things she'd done. "Then will you hurry and cut it so the rest of us can have some?"

Laughing, he looked at her and winked. "Hand me your plate."

Soon, everyone had their plates full of wonderful food. During the meal, she noticed that Cade kept looking at her. She would always love his dreamy eyes. However, this time she knew exactly what he was thinking. The past few nights had been Heaven on Earth as she and Cade put PJ to bed early only so that they could have private time under the covers of their own bed. She realized that as soon as dinner was over, she would start getting PJ ready for bed.

The thought of what would happen later tonight had her hurrying through her meal. Cade seemed to eat his food a little faster, as well. She didn't mind. After all, she'd never had a real honeymoon before.

And… if Carrie had her way, every night would be a honeymoon for her and Cade… for the rest of their happy lives.

THE END

READERS - You will read about what happens to Rebecca Sterling in my series "Runaway Brides." Her story will be "Dane's Bride." Also, Cade Hamilton's sister (Savannah) and brother (Jacob) will have stories in the "Runaway Brides" series, as well.
https://www.authormariehiggins.com/runaway-brides-series

Blizzard Brides series link –
https://www.amazon.com/gp/product/B08J7D7W23

Join my newsletter and add to your reading collection - https://www.authormariehiggins.com/newsletter

ABOUT THE AUTHOR

Marie Higgins is a best-selling, multi-published author of Christian and sweet romance novels; from refined bad-boy heroes who make your heart melt to the feisty heroines who somehow manage to love them regardless of their faults. She's been with a Christian publisher since 2010. Between those and her others, she's published over 90 heartwarming, on-the-edge-of-your-seat stories and broadened her readership by writing mystery/suspense, humor, time-travel, paranormal, along with her love for historical romances. Her readers have dubbed her "Queen of Tease", because of all her twists and turns and unexpected endings.

Visit her website to discover more about her – https://authormariehiggins.com

Printed in Great Britain
by Amazon